Emily stra

Her chin came up ... st alarming way. "S ... ur on the dance floo ... ou be by my side to help persuade them to our cause?"

There had been a moment when his eyes widened. But it was a very brief one. "My dear Miss Ashbourne, if you meet these men on the dance floor, you will not have the slightest need of my help. Your beauty alone will charm them into doing so."

Emily sighed. "Mr. Langford, do not insult me with meaningless nonsense that not even a baby could pretend to believe. You wish to set me a task you believe impossible. Well, Mr. Langford, I shall not fail. And then you, sir, must either prove a false witness, or do as you have said you would." She had wanted to believe in Mr. Langford. Well, she ought to have known better! "Good day, sir. I shall not trouble you again."

Emily felt a pair of hands grasp her shoulders. His hands squeezed tight, and she held her breath to hear what he would say. "You mistake me, Miss Ashbourne. I do believe this is the best way for you to proceed. And I promise that when you find a way to attend a ball or party, I shall come as well and stand by you."

The Reckless Barrister

by

April Kihlstrom

A SIGNET BOOK

SIGNET
Published by the Penguin Group
Penguin Putnam Inc., 375 Hudson Street,
New York, New York 10014, U.S.A.
Penguin Books Ltd, 27 Wrights Lane,
London W8 5TZ, England
Penguin Books Australia Ltd, Ringwood,
Victoria, Australia
Penguin Books Canada Ltd, 10 Alcorn Avenue,
Toronto, Ontario, Canada M4V 3B2
Penguin Books (N.Z.) Ltd, 182–190 Wairau Road,
Auckland 10, New Zealand

Penguin Books Ltd, Registered Offices:
Harmondsworth, Middlesex, England

First published by Signet, an imprint of Dutton NAL,
a member of Penguin Putnam Inc.

First Printing, April, 1999
10 9 8 7 6 5 4 3 2 1

Copyright © April Kihlstrom, 1999

Prologue

Sir Thomas Levenger regarded his protégé, Philip Langford, England's newest barrister, with some satisfaction. Of the four brothers to whom he stood godfather, Philip was undoubtedly his favorite, and not just because the boy had followed in his footsteps.

Nor was it because he was the most handsome of the lot. James, Harry, and Philip were all accounted to be remarkably good-looking young men. They were tall, with burnished blond or brown hair, and deep gray eyes. Some even said that their older brother, George, Lord Darton, had to be a changeling. He was everything they were not: sober, staid, responsible, and lacking in anything akin to charm.

At the moment, however, the subject was neither Philip's new honors nor Harry's plans to leave for the war in Spain in the morning, nor even James's latest project. Instead they were discussing George and his wife, Athenia.

"She's whelped another boy, I hear," Harry said lightly.

"Oh, God! He'll be just as impossible as the others," James said with a shudder.

"Now, now, let's be fair, he may well be much better," Philip temporized. "George and Athenia may have learned from their mistakes."

James snorted. "They might if they could but be brought to admit to any! You know as well as I that they consider their offspring to be perfect angels."

Harry merely smiled wryly and said, "I know you are

kindhearted, too much so for a barrister in my opinion, Philip, but that does not mean you must concede every point to George. Yes, yes, I know, you mean to rip up at me again but I beg you will not. George and Athenia and their offspring could be everything that is considered proper and admirable and we would still not be able to stand them."

Philip colored and shifted uncomfortably in his chair. "Perhaps it is marriage. A great many people, I believe, become more staid once they settle into marriage.

"A good reason for us to never fall into that trap," Harry countered.

"Look at Sir Thomas. He's happy. Aren't you, sir?"

"I am," Sir Thomas agreed gravely. "But that does not mean all men are suited to the single state."

"We are," Harry said firmly.

"I know!" James chimed in. He raised his glass and the others fell silent. "I propose a vow," he said. "Why don't we, all three, promise each other never to marry and, moreover, to stop the others from doing so if we should ever see such a danger in store."

"Hear, hear!" Harry said, raising his own glass in agreement.

Philip hesitated, then shrugged. He lifted his own glass of brandy. Truth to tell, the hour was late and he was as reluctant as his brothers to step into the parson's mousetrap. And it was very much on his mind since he had just come from the Darton estate, where he had been obliged to listen to George lecture him endlessly on his duties and responsibilities and how it was time he gave up this nonsense of studying the law and returned to simply being a gentleman. George had not been pleased to learn he had been called to the bar. Quite the contrary.

And so, at the moment, Philip was in a mood to rebel against every word he had heard there. So now he raised his own glass and, in a voice that was none too steady, said, "Very well. A vow. None of us to marry."

The three brothers clinked glasses and smiled smugly at one another. Sir Thomas merely watched them, a gleam of irony in his own dark eyes and a thoughtful expression on his placid face. That alone ought to have warned Philip.

But Harry was already speaking again. "By the time I return to England, Philip," he said, a teasing note in his voice, "I shall expect you to be King's counsel."

"And shall I expect you to return a general?" Philip shot back.

"We shall at the very least expect you to make your fortune handling the affairs of wealthy clients," James chimed in.

Philip snorted. "I have no cases. Not yet," he countered. "And not likely to have many until I am known. It takes time for that to happen."

Sir Thomas moved his chair and bestirred himself to say, "Oh, I might be able to throw a client or two your way."

"Thank you, you are very kind," Philip replied, after a moment's hesitation.

"But you would rather find your own?" Sir Thomas asked shrewdly. When Philip nodded, it was Levenger's turn to snort. "Come, boy, we all begin by having clients sent our way by those who are looking out for us. Don't be ungrateful!"

It was one of the things Sir Thomas liked best about young Philip that he immediately flushed and stammered an apology. Sir Thomas waved a hand carelessly.

"No, no, I know you didn't mean to be rude, m'boy. But you ought to know there were those who helped me and now it is my turn to help you."

It was Harry who said quietly, "You have helped all of us, a great deal, these past eight years, sir, since our parents were killed. We are all in your debt."

"Nonsense!" Sir Thomas said impatiently. "I was a friend of your father. I have done no more than he would have expected of me!"

Now it was James who smiled sweetly and said, "On the contrary, sir, you have done much more and we know it."

Philip merely looked at his mentor and said, his voice taut with emotion, "You know very well, sir, how grateful I am. And while you will not hear it, you cannot stop us from feeling as we do."

Sir Thomas growled something about impertinent whelps and reached for a deck of cards. "The devil with all of you! Come and let an old fellow teach you a few new tricks. You, Harry, may need them amongst your fellow officers and tonight is my last chance to teach you some before you leave."

Chapter 1

Philip Langford was deep in the perusal of Hale's *History of the Common Law* when there was a rap at the door of his office at Gray's Inn. He looked up with some annoyance at the interruption.

At his command, a clerk poked his head into the room and said, "You've a client, sir. Out here."

"A client?" Philip echoed, a bewildered edge to his voice. "Why don't you show him in?"

"It's a her and I would if I could get her past all the gawkers."

His interest finally engaged, Philip headed for the door, reaching for his coat and pulling it on as he did so. And then he stood in the hallway staring in the direction the clerk was pointing. Just as the fellow had said, there was a woman, a young lady, standing in the central area, asking to speak with him.

He was puzzled by what he saw. She carried herself with far too much assurance to be a servant or a member of the lower or middle classes and yet her dark green dress and pelisse were patently not of the best quality and her bonnet had clearly seen better days. A gentle woman who had fallen upon hard times? Heaven preserve him from such a creature! What did she imagine he could do for her?

At the moment she was surrounded by a number of barristers and would-be barristers offering to help her. But not in the manner she meant. Their raucous comments were clearly distressing the girl and with a sigh Philip realized it was past time that he took a hand in the matter.

"I am Philip Langford and I can see you now," he called out.

The crowd parted around the young woman. He regarded her gravely and she looked at him with some asperity and a singular lack of gratitude which took him aback. Nevertheless he moved closer to her.

"You are much younger than I expected," she said with a frown.

Amused, Philip bowed and said, "I cannot help my age. Does it matter?"

A tiny frown creased her forehead. "No, perhaps not," she acknowledged. "Not if you will listen to me and take my concerns seriously. But if you are so young, then perhaps you are like these others, merely wishing to have a laugh at my expense."

She waved a hand at the circle around her, which had now fallen silent beneath the heat of her obvious contempt. There were a few muttered grumblings at her comments but most wished to hear what she would say next.

Philip almost turned on his heel and washed his hands of the girl. Every instinct told him she was going to be trouble. But he couldn't abandon her. Not when Spencer was headed her way, a gleam in his eye Philip knew only too well and distrusted even more.

So instead of turning his back, he moved closer to the young woman and said quietly, "Why don't we go into my office and talk. I cannot know, until you tell me the trouble, whether I can help you or not, but I assure you, I will not laugh at your expense."

And that should have been that. But it wasn't.

Emily Ashbourne looked up at the man who seemed to tower over her and she felt a distinct sense of alarm. He was trying to reassure her and, to her utter astonishment, it seemed he would succeed. How very strange!

Still, she thought, she needn't let the fellow feel he had the upper hand entirely. He caused the most unsettling sensations in the pit of her stomach when he looked at her as he was right now.

With a coolness she was far from feeling, Emily gripped her reticule tighter and said, "Very well, sir. Lead the way to your office."

That took him aback, she thought with some satisfaction. Around them rose a new chorus of crude jests, but she didn't care and neither, she thought oddly, did he.

It took her by surprise when suddenly he smiled, backed a step away, and bowed to her. And it was such a singularly sweet smile that it all but took her breath away.

Still, Emily was determined not to be cozened so easily. She knew only too well how charming a gentleman could be and she had no wish to encourage this one. Even if he was willing to listen to her.

Her uncle's friend, Sir Thomas Levenger, had vouched for him, and yet there was something that made her hesitate. Why was this gentleman a barrister? Principle, like Sir Thomas Levenger? Need? A mere lark he would give up once he grew bored with the notion of doing something useful?

As though he could read her mind, or rather as though he had misread it, he bowed again and said, with what she would swear was a twinkle in his eyes, "The Honorable Philip Langford, at your service. And yes, I am the scandal of my family."

"Oh, surely it is not quite that bad," she said instinctively, before she could judge the wisdom of such a forward remark. "If a man has no funds, he must do something to make his way in the world."

But he did not seem to take offense. He merely gestured toward his office and Emily moved in that direction. She all but bit her tongue to keep from making any more injudicious remarks. At least from making them out here where there were far too many interested parties who might overhear.

Once in his office, Mr. Langford cleared a chair for Emily, indicated she should be seated, then lounged against the fireplace mantel behind his desk.

"Although I suppose it is entirely irrelevant," he said, gazing at a point above her head, "I am not in want of funds. Were I, my family would not be nearly so upset with my choice of profession. They simply believe that I ought to spend my time in pointless pursuits and I happen to disagree."

Emily tilted up her chin. She was suddenly conscious of the haphazard way she had tied the bow of her hat under her chin and wished she had arranged it more becomingly. Such unfamiliar thoughts made her blush but nevertheless she addressed Mr. Langford in a calm, clear voice.

"Good for you," she said. "I find your attitude admirable."

He looked at her and there was a wryness to the gaze that she found most disconcerting. "Do you?" he asked. "But then, you are patently an eccentric yourself so I wonder how much weight I ought to give your opinion?"

It was said without malice, indeed in an almost reflective tone. But it was enough to set off Emily's temper, not the most gentle, even at the best of times.

She rose to her feet, clutching her reticule tighter than before. "And I have patently made an error," she said and stumbled toward the door. "I shall see if there is anyone else who can help me."

She expected him to make fun of her. She expected him to say something sardonic or cruel. Instead, his voice was oddly gentle as he told her, "No one else will see you, you know. Or if they will, it will be only to determine precisely what sort of woman you might be."

Now Emily whirled around to face him. "And you?" she demanded hotly. "What was your reason for seeing me? To determine, as you say, what sort of woman I might be?"

He came toward her, that oddly sweet smile on his face again. He shook his head. His voice was still gentle as he said, "No. For I already know what sort of woman you are."

He reached out to touch her. She flinched away. But it turned out he only wished to straighten her bonnet. Then he stepped back, as though he understood her agitation.

Ashamed of her instinctive reaction, Emily's own voice was softer than she, or anyone who knew her might have expected, as she asked, "And what sort of woman do you think I am, Mr. Langford?"

Again he gestured for her to sit, retreating to the fireplace mantel once more himself. Only when she had reluctantly done so, did he speak. His words were thoughtful, his eyes far too perceptive for her comfort, and the smile a touch wry.

"You are a woman of passion. Passion," he added hastily before she could object to his choice of words, "for some cause or idea or purpose which you believe in. What that cause or idea or purpose might be, I have no notion, but you have patently devoted yourself to it wholeheartedly. Come, tell me. Is it a young man who is in trouble? Someone you love?"

Fascinated, Emily shook her head.

"A member of your family?"

Again she shook her head.

Now he frowned. "Then what?" he asked himself as much as her, as if it were a puzzle he was determined to solve. "And why come to me?"

But she would not let him puzzle it out. Perhaps, Emily told herself, she was afraid of what else he might perceive about her if she gave him time to try. In any event, it seemed far the safest course simply to tell him.

"You are right, Mr. Langford," Emily said. "I do care,

very deeply, about something. And I wish your help on behalf of someone else."

"Who?"

The word was a harsh demand. Emily ignored it. "Or
rather"—she went on, as if she had not heard him—"on behalf of a number of others, though it may, in some part af-
fect me as well. Or so I hope. The question, Mr. Langford,
is whether or not I can trust you."

He stared at her for a long moment and she had the distinct impression that he was forcing himself not to allow his
jaw to fall open. Had no one ever questioned his trustwor-
thiness before? Probably not. And it would do him good to
have it happen now, Emily told herself with a silent sniff. He
clearly had much too high an opinion of himself. Most men
of his class did.

Finally he spoke and Emily held herself very still, prepared for him to hurl a tirade of abuse at her head. Instead
he leaned forward, uncrossed his arms, and took several
steps so that he was close enough to put his hands on his
desk as he bent toward her.

"May I know your name?" he asked very politely.

"Miss Ashbourne."

"Very well, Miss Ashbourne. May I remind you that you
came to me. Presumably because someone recommended
me. You will note that I have refrained from asking who
played such a trick. But since you were given my name, presumably you were also given assurances as to my character.
If they were not sufficient then what, pray tell, would be?"

He paused expectantly, but before she had time to frame
an answer he went on, "Surely not simply my word. If that
were enough you would already trust me. Do you wish me
to call in a clerk or another barrister to stand warranty for
me?"

Again he paused and again he spoke before she had time
to decide upon an answer.

"But of course there is no reason you should take the

word of any of them if you will not take my own. Unless, perhaps, you have merely taken a dislike to my face? No? What then? Come, Miss Ashbourne, this will not do. Either you trust me or you do not. If not, then I suggest you leave right now for I see no way I can possibly be of service to you."

Perversely that decided her. She began to speak in a low voice, knowing he would have to strain to hear her. But she didn't care. It had taken great effort to get herself here and her energies were all but exhausted. If the Honorable Philip Langford proved unreliable, then so be it. She would simply have to try again with someone else.

"Sir Thomas Levenger recommended you, Mr. Langford, and I have reason to trust his judgment. Very well, you are right. That should be sufficient for me. We have wasted enough time; let us get to the business at hand. I presume you are familiar with the riots in the north?"

He inclined his head. She waited but he did not venture an opinion. And again that made her feel better. Clearly he was a man who at least could pretend to listen before he made up his mind and that put him far ahead of any other man she had met of late.

"They, some of those involved, are friends of mine."

"Then you have a poor choice of friends, Miss Ashbourne, and I find it strange that Sir Thomas should have encouraged you in supporting them. Or perhaps he sent you to me so that I could persuade you to abandon them?"

Emily rose to her feet and put her own hands on the desk. Her nose was a scant few inches from his as she said, "Indeed, Mr. Langford? And why do you consider it a poor choice? Why do you think I should abandon them? I cannot. I object, as they do, to machines that are dangerous. What is so terrible in that?"

"I object to your friends because they oppose progress and are willing to resort to violence to prevent it," he countered harshly.

"Calumny!"

"Is it?" he asked, straightening, as if unwilling to face her so closely anymore. "Then how did so many people get hurt?"

"They were hurt," Emily protested, "because the men trying to stop them were cruel."

He opened his mouth then closed it again. He also closed his eyes and squeezed the bridge of his nose with his thumb and forefinger.

When he opened his eyes again, he asked wearily, "And what did you, or Sir Thomas, suppose that I might be able to do on behalf of your friends?"

"Tell us how to change the laws."

"What?"

The word came out almost as a squawk of protest. He gaped at her, he positively gaped. Emily took advantage of his surprise. She pressed her point before he could have time to object.

"You heard me correctly, sir. I wish to know how the law might be changed."

"Which law?" he asked, patently bewildered.

"The law which states that mill owners have the right to do as they wish with their mills in England, regardless of the cost or danger to those they employ, of course," she replied, just as though she believed he ought to understand without her even saying a word.

He was not, she could see, best pleased.

Chapter 2

Trouble. Philip Langford prided himself upon avoiding trouble. Unlike his father who had actively sought it out. And now here he was with a young woman in his office, a young woman who wanted him to tell her how to change the law. What on earth was Sir Thomas thinking, sending her to him? When he saw him, he would have to remember to ask, Philip thought grimly.

Meanwhile, Miss Ashbourne wanted to change the law. That was all. Just change the law. And Sir Thomas had apparently encouraged her in this nonsense. Well, he was as idealistic as his father had been, but that did not mean Philip had to be an equal fool. He clenched his teeth and clasped his hands behind his back. He leaned back on his heels. He stared at Miss Ashbourne. He even smiled at her. Through his clenched teeth.

Finally, when he had command of his voice again, he said, "Sit down, Miss Ashbourne."

She was so astonished at his peremptory tone of command that she did as he said, and then seemed surprised to find herself in the chair. She started to rise again but he gave her no chance. He came around his desk and stood over her so that if she had tried to stand, she would have to come in intimate contact with his body.

"Miss Ashbourne. You speak of changing the law as if it were a little thing. Something to be done at the whim of any gentleman or lady who so chooses. Well, it is not! It is a liv-

ing thing which has evolved in the way that best suits our
nation."

She had courage. He had to give her that. Even as he
stood towering over her, Miss Ashbourne fought back. Her
voice trembled with patent outrage as she replied.

"I do not think it a little thing, Mr. Langford. I know full
well what I ask. But it must be done. The law, which even
you concede evolves and changes, does not best suit our nation. It best suits a few men who either by virtue of their
birth or their good fortune in acquiring property, have the
means to influence those who make and change the laws. It
does not best suit the vast majority of people who live in this
country and are abused in the name of the law every day of
their lives!"

Philip could not deny the tug of sympathy he felt toward
what she said. It was no more than he had thought himself,
upon occasion. Still, his father had been just such a foolish
idealist, taken advantage of time and time again, his parents
ostracized by their friends for his outspoken views. Philip
had watched it all and vowed to be far more clear-headed
when it was his turn. And he was. Now he wanted to shake
the girl and make her realize just how impossible her notions were.

And yet, despite himself, Philip envied her passion, her
conviction. He wished, just for a moment, that he possessed
a little of her certainty. He also, he discovered, perversely
wanted to pull her into his arms and kiss away the anger and
see if there was any other sort of passion behind those wide
blue eyes.

But it was all nonsense! Philip shook his head to dismiss
these odd thoughts. He must be cruel in order to be kind, he
decided. He had to cure Miss Ashbourne of this obsession
before it truly landed her in the briars. He began to clap.
Slowly. Sardonically. With no way to mistake his sarcasm
when he finally spoke.

"Bravo, Miss Ashbourne. You could be making speeches

in Parliament. If you were a man. But you are not. And these are matters best left to men."

He braced himself for her response.

"Men!"

She snorted her disgust. Philip felt his sympathy shrivel. He raised his eyebrows.

"You have something against men, Miss Ashbourne?" he asked politely.

She closed her eyes. And slowly opened them again. Then she rose to her feet and it was Philip who gave way, at the last moment, so that they did not touch one another.

She had fire in her eyes, did Miss Ashbourne. Not by one jot did she seem to be intimidated by anything he had to say. Nor did she seem to care that tendrils of blond hair were escaping her bonnet.

Again she spoke without the slightest trace of hesitation in her voice. "Have I anything against men, Mr. Langford? Indeed, I do. Most of the men I know are fools! They are far less well-informed on matters than I am. And yet I am expected to defer to them and to their opinions simply by virtue of their having been born men! Surely, sir, you cannot expect me to like it?"

Philip could not resist. Without the slightest quiver of laughter in his voice, or trace of smile on his face, he said, "I begin to see, Miss Ashbourne, why you are still Miss Ashbourne."

He thought she would rise to the bait. But she did not. Instead she swallowed hard, tilted her chin upward, and said, "That is a matter for another day's discussion, Mr. Langford. The subject at hand is changing the law. And as much as I dislike having to put so important a matter in the care of a man, it seems I have no choice."

Philip reached out. She flinched and took a step away from him. He let his hands fall to his side. He drew in a breath and said, in even, measured tones, "Miss Ashbourne, I do not know how to convey any more clearly to you that what you ask is impossible. Please let me escort you to your carriage and send you home. You must have family who are worried about you."

"My family is none of your concern and I did not come in my own carriage. I walked."

"You walked!" Philip demanded, taken aback. "Where, then, is your maid? Surely she should be in here with us?"

"I did not bring a maid. Or a footman. Or any other sort of encumbrance. I simply came myself and yes, I walked. When I am ready to leave, I shall walk home again."

Now he understood what he was dealing with and Philip let out a sigh of relief. The poor girl was mad, simply mad. She must have escaped from her family and it would be only right and proper that he return her to them. That must be why Sir Thomas had sent her to him. If, indeed, he had. It was because he could trust Philip to look out for the girl if she managed to slip her keepers and come looking for a barrister. For Philip had no doubt she would have done so even had she not had a recommendation from Sir Thomas.

Now that he understood, Philip was able to keep his voice gentle, and even kind, as he said, "Come, Miss Ashbourne, I shall escort you home. You must be tired."

She regarded him with some asperity. "I am not tired, Mr. Langford. I wish to talk about the law!"

"And so we shall," he agreed, spreading his hands wide. "We shall talk in the carriage as I take you home."

Suddenly a hint of humor lit up her eyes and she said, tilting her head to one side, "Aren't you afraid that it will look most improper, Mr. Langford?"

"Nonsense!" he said heartily. "It is no more than I would do for any of my clients."

"I see. Very well, if it is the only way I can get you to discuss legal matters, then so be it. Shall we go, Mr. Langford?"

He bowed and silently congratulated himself on handling the situation so neatly. He would have her home in a trice.

And then she would be the responsibility of her family again and not his.

So caught up was he in these self-congratulatory thoughts, that Philip almost walked straight into Miss Ashbourne as she paused in his doorway.

She looked up at him as she said dryly, "You may escort me home, Mr. Langford, but any attempt to divert our journey by way of Bedlam will result in great anger, on my part, and prove futile on yours."

And then, before he could even begin to collect his thoughts sufficiently to answer, she turned on her heel and pushed open the door. Philip made haste to follow her.

Men! Emily thought scathingly. Stupid, stupid men! But they were the ones with all the power. It was really most unfair.

And yet, she could not deny that it was a comfort to have Mr. Langford, as provoking as he was, by her side as they passed through the outer office and the courtyard. She was met by even more jeers than when she arrived and she shuddered to think what it would have been like had she had to run this gauntlet without his support.

Indeed, Mr. Langford seemed to have the trick of quelling the wildest of the lot with a quirk of his eyebrows and a quick shake of his head. Emily did not begin to understand how he could do so, but she was grateful nonetheless.

And certainly he had no difficulty hailing a carriage to drive them back to her lodgings. Which was a bitter contrast to her own useless efforts some hours before.

Ought she to admit to Mr. Langford that she had walked to his office out of necessity? Or let him continue to think her so contrary, so determined that she would do almost anything in pursuit of her goal?

Perhaps the latter. It would keep him from thinking he understood her and, in Emily's experience, when a man thought he understood a woman, it was always unfortunate for the poor woman!

Abruptly she became aware that Mr. Langford was regarding her with both impatience and disapproval. "Your direction?" he repeated for what was obviously at least the second or third time.

Emily gave it to him quickly and noted the frown as he recognized she was not lodging in one of the better parts of town. It was, she told herself, none of his affair and she could not, moments later, when they were settled in the hired carriage, understand why she took the trouble to explain.

"I had only been to London once before," Emily said, biting her lower lip. "And I did not stay very long. Certainly not long enough to learn which parts of town were fashionable and which were not."

But it didn't help. Now he regarded her with even more astonishment than before. "Surely it was not," he replied in appalled accents, "your place to choose a lodging, here in London?"

Emily looked away. How honest ought she to be? She was tempted to lie. To say she had mistaken her words. That of course Aunt Agatha had chosen their lodgings.

But when Emily looked again into his clear gray eyes, she found herself telling the truth. "When I decided to come to London I thought it best to present my aunt and my father with a fait accompli. I wrote to a house agent and he sent me a number of suggestions. I hired this house, sight unseen and only then informed my aunt and my father of my plans. And it worked! My father allowed me to come and my aunt accompanied me."

"But such an address!" Mr. Langford persisted.

She didn't have to explain, but somehow Emily found herself doing so. "I thought I had remembered the street we stayed on last time," she said softly, "but it seems I was mistaken."

Emily paused, looked out the grimy window of the hack, and took a deep breath before she continued.

"It was only after we arrived and found the sort of place to which we had committed ourselves that I realized the street I remembered was just a few letters different. But those few letters were the difference between a truly respectable address and shabby gentility."

Again she paused and this time her chin came up in an oddly endearing gesture of defiance. She looked Mr. Langford squarely in the eyes as she said, "But it does not matter, sir, where we are lodged. What matters is what brought me to London. The laws must be changed!"

He spread his hands in a gesture of helplessness and while his expression was carefully neutral, Emily nevertheless had the impression he was laughing at her. His words all but confirmed it.

"But my dear Miss Ashbourne, surely you understand that Parliament makes the laws? I, and my colleagues, are barristers. What could you possibly have hoped to accomplish by coming to me? Why on earth did Sir Thomas think there was any point in you doing so?"

Emily scarcely hesitated. "I hoped to find men, or at least one man, of principle and intelligence. One with knowledge of both the law and the men who make it. I hoped to find someone who would tell me if there were a way to challenge the laws through the courts. And if not, how one might best go about bringing change through the Parliament. Sir Thomas recommended you.

"I was patently misled by the example of my late uncle, who also studied the law and was a good friend to Sir Thomas. He was the most intelligent person, man or woman, I have ever known. And this is just the sort of battle he would have relished. Unfortunately"—cursing her weakness, Emily had to pause to surreptitiously dash a tear from her eyes—"he died two years ago and is not here to help me now."

Before she realized his intention, Mr. Langford took her hand gently in his and said, "I am sorry, Miss Ashbourne. You uncle sounds like a very fine man and I am sorry never to have know him. And sorry he is not here to guide you now. I think even he, however, might have been daunted by what you wish to do."

At these last words, Emily, who had begun to feel unaccountably mellow toward Mr. Langford, felt her temper rise again and she pulled her hand free.

"Perhaps so, Mr. Langford," she said in her most disdainful voice, "but he would at least have had the courage to try to help me. Unfortunately, Sir Thomas neglected to tell me you were a coward."

He flinched as though she had slapped his face and his expression turned cold and harsh. Emily shrank back against the cushions and reflected that perhaps it was not the wisest of moves to insult and provoke a man when one was cooped up in a moving carriage with him.

"My dear Miss Ashbourne," he said evenly, "I regret that I am not able to measure up to this paragon of a man and of a barrister that your uncle apparently was. I can only advise you to concede I, and all of my fellow barristers, are hopelessly flawed and go back to wherever it is you came from before you suffer any further disillusionment and cause any further trouble in the process of doing so!"

Now it was Emily's turn to flinch. To her chagrin she felt her eyes fill with more unwanted moisture. She would not, she vowed, give Mr. Langford the satisfaction of seeing her dash her tears away.

Instead she sat stiffly erect and turned her head as if she found the passing view to be of great fascination. She blinked fiercely, trying to clear her eyes.

Over her shoulder she said, "I shall take your advice under due consideration, Mr. Langford, but I must warn you that I cannot promise to follow it."

That should have done it. That should have been enough

to set a wall firmly between them. Instead Emily heard a muttered curse and then felt two hands grasp her shoulders in a scandalously familiar way and force her to turn and look at Mr. Langford.

For a moment she half hoped, half expected him to make some sort of conciliatory gesture. And there was something else, smoldering in his eyes, that half made her think he meant to kiss her.

Instead he said, biting off each word, "Miss Ashbourne, you are the most provoking woman it has ever been my misfortune to encounter and all I can say is that it is a very good thing we are almost at our destination or I would be tempted to halt the carriage and abandon you here and now."

"Feel perfectly free to do so," Emily said with a dignity that was destroyed by a tiny sound of dismay she could not suppress.

Abruptly he let out his breath and let go of her shoulders. Now he leaned back against the squabs. "No, Miss Ashbourne," he said as he shook his head. "I said I would see you home and I meant it. Once you are in your family's care again you will be, I thank God, no longer my responsibility, in any way!"

Emily opened her mouth to retaliate, but the carriage came to an abrupt halt and Mr. Langford immediately opened the door and hopped out. He turned to hold out a hand to help her down and she could not help thinking, with a sniff of disdain, that it would be very hard to tell which of them was the more relieved to be rid of the other!

Chapter 3

Philip felt his temper to be on a very short rein though, at the moment, he could not have said whether he was angrier at the woman beside him or at Sir Thomas. Fortunately, in moments, he would relinquish Miss Ashbourne and he need never see the provoking creature again. Then he was going to find Sir Thomas and ask what the devil he had been thinking! Philip rapped impatiently on the front door, wondering why the servants were taking so long to answer.

And when someone did finally come, the woman who opened the door bore a marked resemblance to Miss Ashbourne. Her first words confirmed his suspicions and Philip began to wonder if perhaps madness ran in the family.

She peered at him, saying sharply, "Come in, come in. I am Miss Jarrod. No doubt you've come about the bills. I'm afraid I have no head for numbers, but my niece can sort it all out when she returns."

Philip closed his eyes. It only wanted that—to be mistaken for a tradesman!

She made it even worse when she added, with a note of hope in her voice, "Or perhaps you are the applicant for the position of butler?"

A servant? She thought he might be a servant? Philip opened his mouth to give the woman a blistering setdown and felt rather than saw Miss Ashbourne hastily step in front of him.

"Aunt Agatha! If you would but wear your eyeglasses you

would not mistake a gentleman for a servant! Or a tradesman. In any event, what are you doing answering the door?"
she demanded. "Where is Pinkley?"

The older woman waved a hand. "Oh, I sent him off,
Emily. He was drinking the brandy, you know. And stealing
the silver. Which isn't even ours, as the house came fur-
nished. And what we are going to tell the landlord is beyond
me."

But this was all too much for Philip. Bewildered he demanded, unable to suppress a frown, "Have you no other
servants to open the door for you? Must you do so yourself,
Miss Jarrod?"

"Of course we have other servants!" Miss Ashbourne said
indignantly

"Well, no, we don't, Emily," Miss Jarrod said, turning a
bit pink.

Miss Ashbourne regarded her aunt with patent bewilder-
ment. "Why not?" she asked.

"Pinkley took them with him when he left," Miss Jarrod
replied hotly. "He said that if I would not keep him on, he
would not let me keep the others either. And I couldn't, not
when he was a thief! Oh, Emily, what are we to do? I went
to an agency and asked them to send round some more servants right away, but they said they couldn't promise anything and none have come."

Miss Ashbourne went very pale. She closed her eyes for
a moment and seemed to murmur something under her
breath. Philip suspected it was as well that none of them
could hear what she said.

Then Miss Ashbourne opened her eyes again and there
was a kind of sad resignation in them as she said, "Come
along, Aunt Agatha. We shall have to go and hire more servants. But meanwhile we must not stand on the front stoop
providing entertainment for the entire street."

It was as though she had forgotten him, Philip thought as
he followed her inside. The moment the door closed behind

him, however, he realized his mistake. Miss Ashbourne apparently only wished for a bit of privacy before she ripped up at him. And now she did so with a vengeance

"Mr. Langford, I thank you for escorting me home and now you may go. I am very sorry to have troubled you and taken up your valuable time to no purpose. I shall not make such a mistake again."

Good, Philip thought. The last thing he needed was such an odd creature, and her even odder aunt, complicating his existence. Which is why he was so surprised that, instead of turning and leaving, he took a step closer to her and said, "Let me hire some servants for you, Miss Ashbourne. I promise they shall be more reliable than the ones you've been saddled with, heretofore. They shan't be thieves and they won't desert you without a moment's notice."

She started to refuse and he knew he should let her, honor satisfied. Instead he spoke before she could even begin to frame a reply.

"Please, Miss Ashbourne! I assure you I know London far better than you do and any servants you try to engage will be the worst sort, for the agencies will think they can take advantage of you and your aunt."

She wanted to refuse. He could read it in her eyes. But just as he had acted against what his common sense told him, so now did she act against what he saw in her face.

She took a deep breath and said, "I should be very grateful to you, Mr. Langford, if you would. I know I should not put myself under such an obligation to you. I know that I have troubled you far too much already. But I confess I am at my wit's end and should be grateful to have your assistance. Only I must warn you, one reason we have this problem is that we cannot afford to pay these London servants as well as they seem to expect."

Instantly Philip made his decision. She would have her servants and they would be reliable ones. And they would cost her no more than she could afford. She would also never know why that was so.

Afraid she might read something of his intentions in his eyes, he bowed and said, "I understand and will take that circumstance into account. And now you must excuse me. I had best go at once for I strongly suspect that if you wish dinner tonight there is no time to be lost."

And then she smiled up at him, the sweetest, most wistful smile Philip had ever seen. Unlike the young misses who came to London each Season, she made no effort to hide her emotions. Indeed, her voice trembled as she thanked him.

"You are much too good, Mr. Langford, and I most deeply regret castigating you before."

Because he didn't know what to make of a woman who did not hide her true nature, Philip escaped without answering. Behind him he could hear Miss Jarrod ask in a suspicious voice, "Where is he going, your young man, Emily? Oughtn't you to invite him into the parlor? Mind, we would have to clear some books off of the chairs, but still one ought to make the effort."

And as the door closed behind him, Philip just heard the beginning of Miss Ashbourne's soothing reply.

"He will perhaps come another day, Aunt Agatha. He had an urgent appointment. Meanwhile, come and sit in the drawing room. I . . ."

Philip smiled to himself. No doubt she had said what she did only to pacify her aunt. But Miss Ashbourne would soon discover that her words were more correct than she guessed. He would call again and he would see this infamous parlor for himself. And then, perhaps, he could shake this odd spell Miss Ashbourne seemed to have cast over him.

God forfend any of his friends or worse, his brothers, should discover that he, Philip Langford, had undertaken to procure servants for a spinster like Miss Ashbourne!

Despite himself, he found himself wondering what she would do next, for he did not believe she would simply abandon her cause. Attempt to storm Parliament? She might if it were in session, but it was not.

Approach members of the House of Lords? She would get short shrift if she did. And while there were a number of men in the House of Commons who might be sympathetic to her cause, Philip could not, in good conscience, place her in their company. Indeed, he shuddered at the thought.

Still he could not believe, even with these obstacles before her, that Miss Ashbourne would give up. Not when she had the sort of passion that Sir Thomas was always telling him he ought to have. But he didn't.

Suddenly Philip thought he understood why Sir Thomas had sent Miss Ashbourne to see him. Well, if he thought to influence Philip that way, he would soon find he was mistaken. If Miss Ashbourne's behavior today was any indication of the foolishness one could be driven to by such passion as Sir Thomas was forever telling him he needed, Philip did not wish to have any part such a thing.

Abruptly Philip shook himself. It was absurd to waste any more time thinking about the young woman! He would help her find servants, but that was all. She was not his concern, even if Sir Thomas had sent her to him. And so he would tell his mentor when next he saw him. Miss Ashbourne's father ought to be watching over her!

Philip paused, trying to recollect whether he had heard of any Mr. Ashbourne who was accounted a fierce reformer, but the name conjured up no such picture. Certainly he could not recall his father ever mentioning the man. Still, he must be, or how else would he come to have such a firebrand for a daughter? Philip shuddered and hoped he would never meet the fellow. One Ashbourne with a zeal for reform was far more than enough for his tastes.

He found himself wondering when Miss Ashbourne had come to London before and what havoc she had wreaked when she did so. He ought to have asked her, but that would only have served to strengthen the connection between them, something he was most eager to avoid.

Or so he thought. Still, he wondered. Perhaps James would know. He seemed to know all the on-dits, the crim-con, and so forth. But only about the *ton*, Philip acknowledged. He was unlikely to know about one eccentric young woman who had probably never set foot in a ballroom in her life.

Sir Thomas. Yes, that was it. Once he had this matter of the servants taken care of, Philip would call upon Sir Thomas. His mentor could surely tell him everything there was to know, everything he ought to know about Miss Ashbourne. And when he was done, Philip would tell him just what he thought of his mentor for serving such a trick upon him!

Emily knew only too well what sort of impression Aunt Agatha had made upon Mr. Langford. It happened all the time. Very few looked beyond the surface appearance to realize that the woman had a shrewd mind and sharp temper. Emily often thought her aunt cultivated such an appearance on purpose, for it served to put so many off the scent. She appeared harmless and sadly shatter-brained and so she was generally allowed to do precisely as she wished.

For if Aunt Agatha had one failing, it was a singular lack of resolution. It had caused her to do as she was told all her life. And while she might aid and abet her niece, secretly, in disobeying her father, she would never do so openly. Nor would she do so unless she could at least pretend to herself that she did not know what was going on.

Aunt Agatha was, Emily thought sadly, a woman torn between duty and rebellion and, unfortunately, duty almost always won. And so she pretended to a vacuity that was not real so that she would be left alone and could do as she wished.

Emily had no patience for such a pretense for herself and,

today it rubbed her the wrong way that Mr. Langford had so easily been taken in by her aunt. Perhaps that was why she was so short with Aunt Agatha over the matter of how she had treated the fellow.

"I don't understand," Agatha said impatiently. "In my day a gentleman was always brought into the drawing room. And just where have you been? You know your father believes you to be here purchasing your wedding clothes. But nothing will make me believe that young man works for a modiste."

"No, he does not!" Emily snapped at her aunt.

"Then why were you with him? It is not at all the thing," Aunt Agatha protested.

Abruptly the defiance went out of Emily. She knew her aunt was doing her best to look out for her. "No, of course not," she said soothingly. "At least not in general. But I encountered some incivility, while I was out, and Mr. Langford was kind enough to come to my aid. Besides, he is a friend of Sir Thomas Levenger and you know how unexceptionable he is!"

"Not to your father," Miss Jarrod said dryly. She paused and peered nearsightedly at her niece but her voice was not in the least vague as she said, "What is going on, Emily?"

"Nothing."

Agatha shook her head. "No, of course not. Nothing is going on. You are the picture of innocence, Emily, but it just won't do. I know you far too well. You are evading my questions and I won't have it."

"Won't you?" Emily countered with a fond smile, for she knew her aunt very well. "Do you truly wish to know what I am about? If you did, you might have to tell Papa."

That halted Aunt Agatha. She sighed. "I ought not to let you do this, Emily. But no one ever has been able to keep you in hand. I confess it is one of the things I like best about you and I am not about to begin to try now. Yes, you are right. I do not wish to know what is going on, after all. Just tell me that I may write to your father that your gowns are ordered and we expect to return shortly."

Emily turned away and pretended to study the scene outside the window. As it was a particularly grim one, however, she fooled neither herself nor her Aunt Agatha.

"I am waiting, Emily."

Over her shoulder, Emily debated how to answer her aunt. Finally she sighed and admitted, "No, Aunt Agatha, my gowns are not ordered. I saw nothing I liked this afternoon. I shall just have to try another day."

And that was the truth, Emily told herself defensively. She hadn't seen any gowns at all, and therefore none that she liked.

"Emily Ashbourne, you do intend to order your trousseau, do you not?" Aunt Agatha asked sternly.

This was the moment to admit that she did not. That indeed, she did not intend to be married at all. But somehow Emily could not bring herself to distress her dear aunt so deeply.

Instead, she said lightly, "You are so suspicious, you and Papa. I cannot understand why."

"Because we know you only too well," Agatha retorted tartly. "At least I do. I've no doubt your papa is still blissful in his belief that you will be the dutiful daughter and wed where he tells you. Though why he should think you would prove dutiful after twenty-three years of fighting him at every turn is beyond me."

Emily smiled wistfully. "Papa believes that which he wishes to believe, that which is useful to him to believe. Even when it must go against all common sense."

Now Agatha wailed. "I knew it! You have as good as admitted you are fooling your father. And what it will come to, I cannot say. He will blame me, I know he will. He will say I should have done better to keep you in hand and the worst of it is, he will be right."

This was the time to remind Aunt Agatha that it was she

who had given her niece Mary Wollstonecraft's *Vindication of the Rights of Woman* and other such books to read. Books that could not help but make Emily reluctant to value propriety more highly that it deserved. But such a reminder would only have distressed her aunt and she was right that Papa would blame Aunt Agatha.

That brought a pang of guilt to Emily. She turned and hugged her aunt. "It will all come about," she promised. "Now, come, sit. Let me make some tea. I do hope Mr. Langford will be able to find us servants today. Reliable servants. I am growing very tired of having the household always at sixes and sevens."

Perhaps because she, too, was skilled at self-deceit, Agatha Jarrod allowed herself to be persuaded, allowed herself to believe that perhaps everything would be all right, after all.

Chapter 4

Philip Langford never intended to set a spy in Miss Ashbourne's household. Indeed, he would have recoiled at the thought of doing so deliberately.

But it proved far more difficult than he anticipated to find servants for the two ladies on such short notice. And in the end, he provided them with a butler by choosing one of his footmen and telling the fortunate fellow of the elevation of his status. The footman was puffed up with pride until he saw the establishment he was to rule over. And then it took all of Philip's powers of persuasion, and a raise in salary, to get him to go in.

Which brought up another point. Somehow Philip had not realized just how expensive servants could be. Reliable servants, at any rate. To be sure, he had a staff of his own and he was vaguely aware of how much he disbursed each year paying them, he just had not thought about it, consciously, for some time.

Philip was uncomfortably aware that the two ladies almost certainly could not afford the staff he engaged on their behalf. And so he found himself promising to pay half their wages himself provided they gave not a hint to the ladies that he was doing so.

He was mad. That was the only possible explanation. Whatever had caused Miss Ashbourne's derangement of mind must have infected him as well. Philip could think of no other reason he was behaving this way.

Well, the obvious solution was to keep as far away from Miss Ashbourne as possible and pray that his own fit of madness would soon run its course.

So why, then, was he driving up to their door, a few days later, in his brother's borrowed phaeton, about to ask Miss Ashbourne if she wished to go out driving? He ought to be in chambers. Or running to ground Sir Thomas, who was proving exceedingly skillful at evading Philip.

Perhaps that was why he was short with the groom as he handed over the reins and climbed down. And perhaps that was why he rapped with unnecessary force on the front door. It was opened immediately by his former footman, who looked taken aback.

"Sir?"

"Announce me, please," Philip said shortly.

The fellow recovered quickly and motioned for Philip to wait while he went to see if the ladies would see him.

As he stood in the foyer, Philip looked around, thinking the place looked even shabbier than it had a few days before. The dark paneling gave the foyer a gloomy feel and the furniture looked as though it was the mismatched castoffs of a number of better endowed households.

Which only made Philip question his sanity even more for being here. Fortunately, he had only a short time for reflection before the former footman returned and said, "Miss Jarrod and Miss Ashbourne will be pleased to see you, if you will step this way."

"Well done, Whiten," Philip said softly. "I thought you would make a good butler."

The footman, now butler, did not reply. Still, he betrayed his gratification at the compliment by the way he colored up beet red above his collar.

The moment he entered the drawing room, however, Philip forgot his former servant. Instead he stood, gaping openmouthed at Miss Ashbourne while she blushed becomingly and Miss Jarrod looked from one to the other in clear approval. This time the older woman was wearing her eye-glasses, a circumstance for which he could only be grateful.

Still, the cause for Philip's astonishment was Miss Ash-bourne's transformation from the shabby genteel young lady who had sat in his office a few days before to a young lady dressed in the first mode of fashion today. Or, rather, not precisely the first mode of fashion, for it was at least a year or two out of date, but it was sufficiently flattering to Miss Ashbourne that few would cavil at such a point.

Indeed he blinked as though to clear the image that could not possibly be real. Then she spoke, and the fashionable young lady was, once again, the sharp-tongued harpy he had met a few days before.

"Ought I to be flattered, Mr. Langford, that I am so transformed beyond recognition for you? Or insulted that you did not think me capable of looking like this?"

"Emily!" Miss Jarrod protested. "How can you speak so to Mr. Langford, after all his kindness to us? You know we should never have found such excellent servants on our own!"

Miss Ashbourne blushed again, but this time with patent mortification. Her voice was stiff as she said, "My aunt is right, Mr. Langford. Pray forgive my wretched tongue and accept our profound gratitude for finding us such an excellent staff. And with such dispatch."

It was clearly a perverse flaw in his nature, Philip thought, that he found he preferred the impetuous Miss Ashbourne who said precisely what she thought, to this pale, albeit beautiful, imitation who parroted polite phrases at her aunt's command.

Still, he was not such a fool to say so aloud. Instead he bowed to her and to Miss Jarrod and replied, in his cool, well-bred voice, "It was a mere trifle. I am pleased to have been of service."

As if that wasn't as pompous as her polite words had been shallow! Philip wanted to kick himself.

Something must have shown on his face, for abruptly Miss Ashbourne came forward and took his hand in hers. There was an impish gleam in her eyes as she said, "Now that we have both said all that is proper, may we be honest? My aunt and I truly are grateful. But you needn't have looked at me, when you came in, as though I had grown a second head!"

She would have let go his hand as she finished speaking, but he would not let her. Instead he grasped her hand and held it tight despite her discreet efforts to pull it free.

He smiled down at her with a warmth that would have dismayed Philip had he realized how thoroughly he betrayed himself. As it was, he said, oblivious to the effect of his smile upon Miss Ashbourne, "It is I who ought to apologize. It is just that you are such a beauty and I had not guessed. I am realizing I must be a far greater fool than I thought possible not to have noticed that first day."

Now she did manage to pull her hand free. "No one was meant to notice," she told him dryly. "I know you thought me foolish to go out alone, but I was not so foolish as to do so looking like this, where I would draw even more unwelcome attention than I did. I meant to look as plain as possible and it would seem I succeeded."

He had to allow the wisdom in her words. Once again it was as though she could read his mind.

"Just so," she said. "And now, if you are done, we shall not force you to stay any longer. You have satisfied the proprieties, indeed, the niceties with your morning call and we shall not hold you to any further obligation."

"Emily! You sound as if you are forcing the poor man out the door!" Miss Jarrod said in scandalized tones. "And after he has been so kind to us!"

Philip looked over to the older woman and smiled reassuringly. "Don't worry," he said, "I am not so easily dislodged. Nor," he went on, turning back to Miss Ashbourne, "did I come merely to pay my respects and satisfy some notion of propriety. I came to ask if you would like to go for a ride in my phaeton."

Instinctively she backed away, shaking her head. Philip frowned. He would swear it was not a conscious action on her part. And her words came in stammered fits and starts, as though she were so overcome with panic she could not think clearly.

"No—that is, I could not impose."

"I am inviting you. It is not an imposition."

"No. It would not be proper. I cannot."

"There is a groom to stand up behind and satisfy the proprieties."

"I cannot. I—I have nothing suitable to wear."

This last was said with hands pressed against her cheeks and Miss Ashbourne's back was against the far wall with nowhere else to retreat.

Philip took pity on her. He kept his voice low and soothing as he said, "Miss Ashbourne, you have nothing to fear from me, I assure you. I only thought you might wish to drive around the park and enjoy the fresh air. Truly I don't care a farthing what you wear."

She wavered. He could see it in the longing in her eyes, in the way she leaned toward him, as unconsciously as before she had backed away.

Careful not to take a step toward her, he threw out what he thought to be an irresistible lure. "We could talk about the laws," he offered. "Surely if you were brave enough to storm my chambers to discuss them, you are brave enough to ride in an open carriage in my company."

"Emily, you didn't!" Miss Jarrod said.

The older woman's scandalized voice betrayed the fact Miss Ashbourne could not have told her aunt where she had been the other day or why. Philip wondered what Banbury tale she had told her aunt to account for his presence by her side when she returned home.

Apparently Miss Ashbourne did not wish to discuss the

matter with Miss Jarrod and chose the lesser of two evils. "I shall be ready in five minutes," she said, scrambling for the drawing room doorway.

Philip bowed and waited until she was gone. Then he sat himself down next to Miss Jarrod and prepared for a cozy conversation with the woman in hopes of learning more about the very odd, the oddly appealing Miss Ashbourne.

Miss Jarrod seemed quite eager to oblige.

Upstairs, Emily once more pressed her hands against the sides of her face. However was she to go back down and face Mr. Langford? And yet if she didn't, she feared he would have no hesitation in coming upstairs and fetching her.

How dare he come and overset her this way? And yet, he had promised to talk with her about the law. Even if he said it to lure her into riding in his carriage, she would hold him to that promise. Despite his discouraging words the other day, there had to be a way to challenge conditions in the mills and factories all over England. Conditions that could only be called scandalously unfair.

And even if it meant riding in a carriage with Mr. Langford, well, Emily had come to London with a purpose and it was a purpose she meant to fulfill.

Taking a deep breath, Emily scrambled to get ready to drive out with Mr. Langford. She was back downstairs no more than five minutes later than she had promised and it was, she discovered, none too soon.

He sat next to Aunt Agatha with his head bent close to hers. Emily could only imagine what her aunt might be telling him and she shuddered. It would be best if she got him out of here as swiftly as possible before Aunt Agatha said anything fatal to her plans.

"Mr. Langford? I am ready," Emily said from the doorway.

At once he was on his feet, coming toward her, offering

her his arm and Emily had to steady herself not to shrink back. But still her fingertips trembled slightly as she touched his sleeve.

He didn't seem to notice and after a moment Emily let out her breath in relief.

She also felt relief that he treated her with cool, distant respect. Which ought to have been precisely what she wished. But, perversely, Emily felt a twinge of disappointment. Where was the man who had met her, insult for insult, point for point? She had never liked popinjays and she was not about to start now.

The fact that Mr. Langford was dressed soberly and acted not in the least like the heedless youth she knew back home was irrelevant. If he mouthed polite nothings, as he was doing right now, she had no interest or respect for him. Still, she supposed it was safer than if he asked questions she had no wish to answer.

And so Emily reassured herself that everything would be all right, after all. How little she knew men. How little she knew herself!

Chapter 5

The ride began reasonably enough. Indeed, how could it not when it was a remarkably fine day for this time of year? Despite her fears, Emily could not help but smile as she stepped out into the bright sunshine.

Mr. Langford helped her into the carriage and went around to the other side. At a discreet signal, the groom let go of the horses' bridle and leaped up onto the back of the carriage. Then they were off, sweeping neatly away from the curb.

"What excellent cattle!" she said.

But he did not seem pleased. "They belong to my brother," he said with some chagrin. At her look of surprise, he unbent sufficiently to add, "I have no need to keep a carriage and James is kind enough to let me borrow his whenever I wish."

"Of course," Emily said, though more to reassure him than anything else.

And then he proceeded to show her that he knew how to drive to an inch. After just a few minutes Emily knew she need not fear he would overturn them.

"You are an accomplished whip," she said approvingly.

Mr. Langford shrugged. "Not nearly so accomplished as I might wish," he countered. "My work as a barrister does not leave me time for it. Are the men you know, back home, so cow-handed then?"

Emily looked away in confusion. Was Mr. Canfield cow-handed? Upon reflection, she thought perhaps he was. One more charge to lay against him, as if she did not have enough already.

But perhaps it was best not to think of that. When one was bound to a man, honor bound to marry him, perhaps it was best to think only of his good qualities. If only, she thought gloomily, she could think of any.

"A farthing for your thoughts," Mr. Langford said gently.

Emily started and realized they were already some distance away from her lodgings. And that Mr. Langford was looking at her with patent concern in his fine gray eyes.

"I was thinking about what you said. About the law," she lied. "And wondering if matters could truly be as hopeless as you seem to think."

He sighed. He distinctly sighed. Had he thought he could divert her from the reason she had agreed to come along? Emily stiffened, angry that he might have done so. And she waited, curious to see how he would answer her.

"Very well, Miss Ashbourne," he said, "we shall discuss the law."

And they did so. Mr. Langford bent every persuasive force he possessed to try to convince her that her mission was hopeless. That it would be too difficult, nay, all but impossible, to persuade Parliament to change the laws as they pertained to mill and factory owners. He tried to persuade Emily that no judge would dare to intervene in so important a matter.

"But that is precisely when they ought to intervene!" she replied with sharp frustration. "If it were an unimportant matter I should not care. What about Sir Thomas? He is a judge."

Mr. Langford sighed and said with little patience, "Even he must be bound by the law. Besides, I do not understand. Was there not a law passed about ten years ago, the Factory Act, which is supposed to protect workers?"

Emily snorted. It was a very unladylike gesture, but she did not care. "Yes, and it is grossly inadequate!"

But they were turning into the park and Mr. Langford had to divert his attention from her to managing his high-spirited horses as they joined a throng of other carriages.

Finally, however, he could speak again with Emily. She listened with amusement as he chose to try a different approach this time.

"How, Miss Ashbourne, do you know what conditions are in these mills and factories? From what your *friends* tell you?" He stressed the word disdainfully. "How do you know they do not exaggerate in order to draw your sympathy and attention? Isn't it unfair to judge what conditions might be solely on the basis of their word?"

Nettled, she replied, "No, Mr. Langford, I do not judge solely on the words of my friends. I tell you the conditions in the mills are horrible because I have seen them with my own eyes."

Now he stared at her with open disbelief and even greater disapproval. In shocked tones he said, "My dear Miss Ashbourne, surely you are not trying to gammon me into believing your family would have allowed you to enter and wander about a mill or a factory? Indeed, I cannot conceive that they would allow you to go anywhere near one! Or that if they did, the owner would let you run tamely about, making no effort to hide conditions if they were as deplorable as you say."

"Well there you are out!" Emily retorted hotly. "I have indeed been inside a mill. And seen at close hand just what goes on there. Nor did Mr. Canfield, the owner, make any attempt to hide conditions from me. So far from doing so, he bragged of how hard he worked his people! And how little he paid them for their efforts."

Mr. Langford frowned, but at least he did not dismiss her comments entirely out of hand. Slowly he asked, "Now why would this Mr. Canfield be so obliging as to

show you over his mill? And why would your family let
you go?"

The question should not have been unexpected. Nor her
answer so difficult to give. But it was. Emily found herself
wishing there were some way to evade Mr. Langford's
piercing gray eyes as they studied her face while he waited
for her answer.

Finally she took a deep breath and said in a rush, "Because Mr. Canfield wished to prove to me how well he could
provide for me once we are married and my father let me go
because he wished me to be persuaded that this marriage is
to my benefit."

"Marriage!"

Mr. Langford echoed the word as though thunderstruck.
And he flinched, palpably flinched, pulling the reins up
short as he did so, causing the horses to jibe in their traces.

He cursed and then he glared at her. "You are roasting
me!"

In a small voice Emily said, "Surely it is not such a
strange notion? Many women my age are already married.
Often with a child or two. Am I such an antidote you cannot
conceive that I should wish to be married as well? Or that
any man should choose to marry me?"

"That is not what I meant and you very well know it!" he
countered irritably as he strained to bring his horses back
under control.

Wide-eyed, Emily stared at him. "Is it not?" she asked,
bewildered. "But if that is not what you meant, then why
should you be surprised?"

He gave up. With another muttered curse, he pulled his
horses to a halt, ignoring the angry driver behind him, and
said with no little exasperation, "Because you are a lady.
Whatever your financial situation, you are a lady. And Mr.
Canfield is patently not a gentleman, if he owns and runs a
mill and can think of no better way to impress you with his
qualities as a husband."

She laughed. She knew it was reprehensible and if her father could see her, indeed if Aunt Agatha could see her, it would mean a scolding, but she couldn't help herself. It was so absurd, so counter to all she had been told these past six months and more, that such considerations seemed ridiculous beyond permission.

She said so aloud.

"It is not in the least ridiculous!" Mr. Langford countered, once again setting his horses going. "I assure you, everyone I know would tell you the same."

Now a grim look crossed Emily's expression. "Then perhaps you, and everyone you know, ought to speak to my father because it is his contention that the match is perfectly unexceptionable."

He stared at her again and Emily wished he would not keep doing so. It was most disconcerting, she thought. An opinion the horses seemed to share, considering the way they suddenly tried to side step in their traces.

"Do you mean to tell me, Miss Ashbourne, that you do not wish for this match?"

Mr. Langford said the words quietly, without inflection, but Emily did not trust the apparent calm. She had the oddest notion that it betokened far stronger emotions than if he had simply shouted the words at her. And therefore she found herself reluctant to answer.

But when he repeated the question for the third time, his voice rising, she knew she had to do so. She finally decided that it would be a relief to be able to tell someone the truth, however much a stranger he might be.

"No, Mr. Langford, I do not wish for this match," Emily said in a level voice.

If her chin was tilted up defiantly, well, that was her business. If her voice held the tiniest quaver, she would not admit to it.

Mr. Langford's response was not in the least what she expected.

"How is he compelling you?" the barrister demanded.

Emily blinked and he repeated the question. Slowly she said, "It is not simply my father. Circumstances compel me as well. My father has only added the weight of his opinion to them."

Once more he stared at her, mouth agape, and once more his horses took exception to this treatment. With a curse, he again halted the carriage, called over his shoulder for the groom to come and take the reins, then leaped down neatly and came around to hand her out.

When Emily hesitated the barrister said in an undertone the groom could not hear, "I do not think we can speak freely in the carriage. Come walk with me a short way along the path."

Emily knew she should refuse. To go would be a mistake. It was foolish. It was just the sort of impulsive action that had caused her misfortune in the first place.

And yet she let him hand her down. She even let him tuck her hand into his elbow as they began to walk, slowly, as if they had all the time in the world. She let him lead her away from the carriage and the crowded path, in a direction that seemed all but deserted.

When they were well away from curious ears, Mr. Langford looked down at her with a kindness that almost undid Emily's carefully erected guard.

"Tell me about it," he invited. "I promise I shall try to understand. And perhaps I can even help you."

There was a tiny lump in Emily's throat as she shook her head, and even she could hear the constraint in her voice as she said, "No one can help me."

"You might be surprised," he countered.

She might have stood proof against that, but when he went on, she was completely undone.

"Please?" he asked, with even greater kindness than before.

Abruptly, the words came tumbling out. "He—we, it

seemed no great harm to go out driving with Mr. Canfield. It was something my papa wished me to do. And it seemed pointless to disoblige him. I never made a secret, to Mr. Canfield, of my unwillingness to marry him."

She paused and drew in air, as though she could not get enough. She fought to find a way to speak the words that would not drive Mr. Langford away.

"Go on," he prompted gently.

There seemed nothing for it but to state the matter baldly, even if it should make him turn away from her in disgust.

"I did not know what he, what Mr. Canfield, intended that day. It began as just another drive. But we did not return until the next morning. Two days later a notice was sent to the papers of our betrothal. And that is why, no matter what you or I or anyone says, I will shortly become Mr. Canfield's wife."

Philip stared down at the young woman beside him, her eyes large in a face that had gone very white. Whatever he had expected, it was not this.

Shaken, he stammered, "I—I am so very sorry for prying into your affairs, Miss Ashbourne. I, that is, of course you must marry him. I had not guessed that you, that he . . ."

Suddenly her expression altered. The color came back into her cheeks and a mischievous gleam lit her eyes. He blinked, taken aback by such an incongruous reaction to such a serious matter. And then she smiled and once more he wondered if she belonged in Bedlam. Had she no notion of the gravity of what she had just told him?

Now she shook her head and looked at him with some exasperation apparent in her eyes.

"Mr. Langford," she said chidingly, "your imagination has run away with you. Mr. Canfield and I did nothing, other than find ourselves to be stranded." She paused, then added with a patent attempt at full honesty, "I grant you that he wished matters to go farther. Had I not found that pitchfork and managed to prove, to his satisfaction, that I meant to use it if necessary, there is no knowing what Mr. Canfield might have tried to do."

Now Philip's hands clenched into fists, as if of their own accord. "I should like to thrash this Mr. Canfield of yours!" he said with a fierceness that astonished him. "He ought not to be allowed to force you into marriage this way."

Miss Ashbourne hesitated and seemed to choose her words with great care. "What other choice have I? He made certain that there would be a great many witnesses to our return. I collect," she said dryly, "that he planned this well in advance."

"You might still have refused," Philip said stubbornly.

"Certainly," she agreed, cheerfully enough, "had I been willing to be thrown out into the street penniless, by my father. For that, you know, is precisely what he threatened to do."

"Is there no one who would have taken you in?" Philip demanded.

Miss Ashbourne shook her head. "No."

Another couple appeared and as one, Philip and Miss Ashbourne decided to start walking again. After a moment, when they had put some distance between themselves and the new couple, Philip asked, "What do you mean to do? It can surely only be misery for you to be married to a man like this Canfield."

Miss Ashbourne halted and looked up at him. "I mean," she said slowly and with great determination, "to destroy his business and prove to him that there could be no worse fate—for him—than to be married to a termagant like myself. And that is the other reason I sought out help to change the mill laws."

He knew he would regret it in the morning. Indeed, he regretted it before the words were even fully spoken. And still, Philip took her hand in his and said solemnly, "Then, Miss Langford, I promise I will help you. Together we shall find a way to persuade Mr. Canfield not to marry you."

Chapter 6

Philip finally managed to run Sir Thomas to ground in his chambers early the next morning before anyone else was about. At the sight of his protégé standing in the doorway to his office, Sir Thomas lifted an eyebrow and gestured him to come in.

"Ah, good morning, Philip. Have you come to discuss the Wentworth case?" Sir Thomas asked as the younger man took a seat.

"I should like to do so," Philip admitted. "But I should also like to ask you about Miss Ashbourne."

"She wrote to you, then?"

Philip drew in a deep breath. "Wrote to me? No, she didn't write. She came to see me. She told me you had sent her. I collect you knew her uncle."

"Her uncle, your father, and I were all friends," Sir Thomas said gravely.

The elder barrister's expression gave no hint of what he was thinking. It was one of the things that made him so successful in court. At the moment, however, Philip found the impassiveness a source of supreme exasperation.

"Do you know what she wishes me to do?" Philip asked, holding on to his temper with an effort.

Sir Thomas shrugged. "She wrote and asked for my help, but without telling me what sort of help she needed, only that she wished the aid of a barrister. I had to reply that I am now a judge but I gave her your direction and suggested she ask you to take the matter in hand. I did not expect her to come to London herself. What, by the by, was the matter she needed help with?"

Philip gritted his teeth. "Oh, a mere trifle. Miss Ashbourne merely wishes to change the laws of England. Those regarding mills and factories. She wishes to protect workers against their employers. And she will not listen to reason, sir!"

"I see." Sir Thomas pursed his lips. Judiciously he said, "It is just the sort of cause your father would have relished supporting, even in the House of Lords."

"My father is dead and George will certainly not do so," Philip countered. "I cannot make Miss Ashbourne comprehend that there is nothing I can do to help her."

"Or nothing you wish to do?" Sir Thomas hazarded shrewdly.

"I am sorry to disappoint you," Philip said stiffly.

Sir Thomas shrugged. "I am not disappointed, precisely. You are still very young—"

"Five and twenty," Philip countered.

"Still very young," Sir Thomas repeated, undaunted. "You have time to grow into your true character. And I have no doubt you will."

"And was sending Miss Ashbourne to me meant to prod me into doing so more quickly?"

"No." Sir Thomas smiled. "I will admit that I hope she does so, but I sent her to you because I am fond of you, you need clients, and I thought the two of you would deal well together."

Philips wanted to refute the suggestion. He want to snort and declare once again the impossibility of Miss Ashbourne's notions. Instead he found a corner of his mouth tugging upward almost into a smile.

"I will allow," he said begrudgingly, "that Miss Ashbourne has made my life much more interesting the past few days. I have learned more than I ever wished to know about hiring servants."

Sir Thomas chuckled. "I shan't ask what that is about, for I can see you won't wish to tell me. I do not ask the impossible of you, Philip, even if Miss Ashbourne does. But I must admit that knowing she is in London, I am glad you will be able to keep a careful eye on her. Perhaps the two of you will even discover you have a great deal in common."

"Miss Ashbourne is here to buy her bridal clothes," Philip said, unable to resist the chance to depress Sir Thomas's obvious matchmaking intentions.

It worked precisely as he hoped. "Bridal clothes?" Sir Thomas sputtered. "What the devil? I have heard nothing of this. Who is she to marry?"

Philip looked at his fingernails, carefully avoiding his mentor's eyes as he said innocently, "A Mr. Richard Canfield, I believe."

"Canfield!"

It was Philip's turn to be startled. "Do you know the man?" he asked.

"I know of him," Sir Thomas answered grimly. "And nothing to his credit! Or rather, very little to his credit. He is a self-made man. He came out of the poorhouse, went to work in a mill, and made himself so useful to the owner that when the fellow died, Canfield inherited everything. He is ruthless, not overly choosy in the means he employs to achieve his goals, gives not a damn about his workers, and is intent upon thrusting himself into society. Hence, I must suppose, his impending marriage to Miss Ashbourne. I cannot imagine two people less suited to one another."

"Neither can I," Philip said curtly. "That is why I have agreed to help her try to find a way out of her betrothal. Canfield forced her into it, you see. With her father's help," he added grimly.

"I think," Sir Thomas said, leaning back with a gleam in

his eye that Philip knew boded ill for Canfield, "that you had better tell me everything."

Philip leaned forward and did so.

In another part of England, the Honorable Mr. Ashbourne stared at the most recent letter from his late wife's sister and tried to make heads or tails of what she was saying. At last he gave it up as a poor job.

They ought to be back already. How long could it take to order a wardrobe, anyway? And why couldn't Emily have done so here? The longer it took before a date could be set for her wedding, the longer before Canfield would fund Mr. Ashbourne's plans for a breeding stable on his land.

Something discreet, of course. Nothing crass, but rather, a place that would be known for a small number of excellently bred cattle. Everything would be handled in the most gentlemanly of ways.

But it all depended on Canfield disbursing the funds. Which he wouldn't do until the knot was safely tied between himself and Emily. And if the girl was the dutiful daughter she ought to be, Ashbourne thought resentfully, she'd be back here by now and ready to marry the man.

His greatest fear was that she would yet cry off, despite the consequences to her reputation. No, she needed to be married and as quickly as possible. Good Lord, the girl ought to be grateful that, past her last prayers as she was, there was a man willing, nay, eager to wed her!

But could she see it? No! It had taken all his authority to override her protests and tears. This trip to London was the one concession she'd manage to wring from him. And he wouldn't have done so if she hadn't used estate funds to pay for the hire of a house so that if he hadn't let her go the money would have gone to waste. He only hoped she wasn't playing out one of her schemes again.

Well, he'd overrule her, if he had to. The moment she returned from London. And if she took much longer about it, he'd go there himself and hurry her in whatever female things it was she thought she had to do.

But that would have meant expense. Expense Mr. Ashbourne was reluctant to bear. Until Canfield placed the promised funds into his hands, he must not spend a farthing more than absolutely necessary.

Which was another reason he begrudged how long Emily and her aunt were taking in London. Why his daughter had hired a house was beyond him. And yet, it was true that to stay in a hotel would have cost almost as much, perhaps even more.

The fact that his sister-in-law, Miss Jarrod, was bearing all expenses herself, save that of the actual hire of the house, did not weigh with Ashbourne. He still begrudged every penny, for otherwise, he persuaded himself, it might have come to him.

With a sigh, he rose from his breakfast and went to go through the accounts yet once again. It ought to be Emily doing so, but since she wasn't here, he would have to go through them and see where expenses might be cut. Something Emily was reluctant to do. Well, perhaps it was a blessing after all that she was not back yet.

Yesterday he had discovered that she had been allowing the purchase of expensive cuts of meat. Surely Cook was skilled enough to make do with cheaper ones? That had been an easy place to make a change and however much Cook protested she would soon accustom herself. But it still was not enough. So Mr. Ashbourne set himself down in his study and pulled the account books forward.

He was lost in the numbers when a rap at the study door startled him. Angrily he called for the servant to enter but, a moment later, rose to his feet, his face wreathed in smiles, his hand held out in welcome.

"Canfield! It is good to see you! What brings you here this fine morning?"

"Is it fine?" Canfield asked with a cool air, ignoring the

hand held out to him. "I had not noticed. I came, sir, to discover when my bride-to-be returns home again."

Slowly, Ashbourne pulled back the rejected hand. Stiffly, he answered, "I do not know, Canfield. I have told you before: ladies take a great deal of time and trouble over their clothes and I would not deny my daughter her right to do so as well. I have had a letter from my sister-in-law and it seems the fittings are taking longer than expected."

Canfield nodded curtly and some of the stiffness left his shoulders. He even condescended to throw himself in the nearest chair. He leaned back and crossed one leg carelessly over the other.

"Ah. Well. Of course. I merely wanted to make certain she was not trying to avoid me."

"Why should she do that?" Ashbourne prevaricated, his color betraying his pretend innocence.

Canfield merely gave him a derisive look and didn't even bother to answer. Instead he smacked one glove against the palm of his other hand and said meditatively, "You do know that my backing for your stables depends on Emily going through with the marriage?"

"Of course!" Ashbourne protested. "And I assure you she will do so willingly."

Again the derisive look. "I do not look for the impossible," Canfield said dryly. "I shall settle for her doing so at all."

"She will!" Ashbourne avowed fervently. "I swear it. She may be headstrong, at times, but in this, I assure you, she will obey me. I have her word. Perhaps if you wrote her a love letter? Perhaps you could remind her of the advantages in being allied to you?"

Canfield considered that. Eventually he nodded. "Yes, I suppose I ought to do so. Emily is a woman and women wish to be pursued. Very well, I shall write such a love letter and send it to her in London. I will even be patient a while longer, Ashbourne. But only a little while longer. I want my wife!"

And with that, Canfield rose to his feet and stalked from the room, not bothering to shut the study door behind him. Ashbourne did not know how it was, but even though he was Canfield's social better, he found himself wiping his brow and, without complaint, closing the study door behind his truculent visitor.

He started to reach for the account books again and changed his mind. Instead he reached for a fresh sheet of paper and a knife to trim his quill. It was time he sent his sister-in-law another letter urging her to return home with all due haste.

In London, unaware of what her father and her suitor were saying, Emily repaired the hem of one of her gowns and found herself wondering if Mr. Langford would come to call again today.

It felt very strange to be thinking of a man in such a way. To feel as though she could trust him to look out for her interests. After all, her father had never done so. Nor Mr. Canfield. But somehow Emily found herself believing Mr. Langford when he said he would help her.

"Emily! You've pricked your finger! Again! And now you've spotted the gown with blood," Aunt Agatha said with pardonable exasperation.

Hastily Emily surveyed the damage. "It is on the inside and does not show through," she assured her aunt.

"Not this time, at any rate," Agatha grumbled. "Whatever are you thinking about that you should be so careless?"

Emily blushed fiercely, and bent her head to hide her fiery cheeks. Aunt Agatha was having none of it.

"Mr. Langford again?" she hazarded shrewdly. "Good! I should like to think you had taken a liking to him. I certainly have! I wonder if we could persuade your father to prefer him to Mr. Canfield? Does he have a fortune, do you think?"

"Aunt Agatha!" Emily exclaimed, scandalized.

"Oh, I shan't say anything of the sort in front of Mr. Langford," Agatha assured her niece. "But one must be practical. And I do much prefer Mr. Langford to Mr. Canfield, don't you?"

Fortunately, the sound of the knocker at the front door forestalled the need for Emily to answer. Though the manner in which she smiled and the blush that came to her cheeks when Mr. Langford was shown into the parlor might well have been considered sufficient answer to Miss Jarrod's question.

Chapter 7

Two days later, Philip found his brother James waiting in his chambers, glancing through some of his law books. Although James was younger by several years, he had the most disconcerting way of looking at one as if he could read one's thoughts. He set aside the book he was holding and gave Philip just such a look right now. There was only one way to handle James when he was in this sort of mood.

"Out with it," Philip said waving his brother to a chair as he took up his post by the empty fireplace. "Why are you here?"

"To discover," James said blandly as he sat down and leaned back to stare up at his older brother, "how and why you have undergone such an astounding transformation that you have been observed dancing attendance upon one young lady. I have heard you have even gone so far as to take her driving in the park. And I am also here to discover what these rumors are of another young lady who is supposed to have invaded your offices a week ago."

Philip considered lying to his brother, but it was too much trouble. Besides, he had no doubt James would soon ferret out the truth, if he tried to do so.

Instead, he made sure the office door was securely closed, then came back and sat down opposite James. He, too, leaned back in his chair.

And in his blandest, most innocuous voice, he said, "Such curiosity! And all for nothing. The young lady, in both cases, is Miss Ashbourne. It seems her uncle was a friend of our father's and when she wrote to Sir Thomas to ask for legal advice, he suggested she come to me. I have merely been looking out for an old family friend."

James quirked an eyebrow. "Taking her out driving? Doing it much too brown, Philip! I cannot recall when you last favored any lady in such a way."

"Miss Ashbourne required my assistance with a matter and rather than allow her to subject herself to the noise and abuse of this office," Philip said stiffly, "I took her out driving in my carriage, or rather your carriage, to discuss whether or not I could help her."

"Can you?"

That was the question, wasn't it? Philip, unfortunately, wasn't at all sure. He said something of the sort aloud. That brought James upright in an instant, his feet landing on the floor in a solid thump.

"Just what the devil do you mean by that?" James demanded.

"Precisely what I said," Philip answered irritably. "Her circumstances are distressing, what she wishes to accomplish unorthodox, and my means to help her quite limited.

James studied his face for a long moment, then leaned back in the chair again. "In that case," he said, waving a hand carelessly, "you had best forget about her altogether. Fob her off on someone else."

"I don't want to fob her off on someone else!" Philip snapped before he could help himself. Then, attempting to retrieve his position he added hastily, "I have told you, Miss Ashbourne's uncle was a friend to Father. Of course I cannot fob her off on someone else."

James grinned. "No, no, you are too late. You have betrayed yourself," he said. "You had best accept that fact and tell me all about Miss Ashbourne. This young lady you cannot bear to send on to anyone else."

Instead Philip directed his own quelling look at James. "I

think," he said, "I should rather hear about your latest exploit. What are you up to now? And does George know about it?"

James blushed, confirming that Philip had planted a flush hit. He waited, knowing that his younger brother would not be able to refrain from telling someone.

"I've been working with this fellow. We made a few modifications to some machinery and well, it's going to be used in one of the largest factories in the north."

Philip grinned. "So you've made some more money?" he asked.

James flushed again and avoided his brother's eyes. His voice was defensive as he said, "I wasn't trying. And you needn't say it so loudly. I should much rather our friends think I'm just tinkering, as I always do. Or won it gambling. That, at any rate, is considered perfectly acceptable."

Philip was no longer grinning. Indeed, his brows were drawn together so tightly that he looked quite fierce. "Has George been at you again? Telling you it's improper for you to earn money? You ought, surely, to know better than to listen to him! What does he expect you to do?"

James looked at his brother unhappily. "He thinks I ought to be a proper gentleman and let him support me for the rest of my life on an allowance. But Philip, I can't! I couldn't be so idle! I should hate it! I've tried gaming, and even now that's where I tell everyone I've made my funds—including George. I promise you I know how to play the perfect gentleman, and I do it very well. But I've got to do something with my days! And I will not become a clergyman, however often George tells me I ought to do so."

"I should think not!" Philip's expression softened. He got to his feet and came around to put a hand on his younger brother's shoulder. "And I do understand your need to be doing something, James. You play the role, by the by, of the dilettante remarkably well. That ought to be enough to satisfy George."

"Thank you. I wish George thought so."

Philip squeezed his brother's shoulder. "I, for one, however, am very glad you are not such a foolish, foppish fellow," he said. "Do as you wish and if George scolds, tell him to come to me. I shall deal with him for you."

N   it was James's turn to look up at his brother and grin. "Peace," he said. "I can handle George. And you are trying to divert my attention, but it won't work. Tell me about Miss Ashbourne. I am all ears and"—he held up a hand to forestall his brother's protests—"consider that if I am to counter the gossip I hear, I had best know the truth."

So, despite the fact that he didn't wish to do so, Philip told his brother everything. At least he told him everything he was willing to admit to in his own heart. And that was only a small part of the whole.

If James guessed this to be the case, he was too discreet to say so aloud. Instead, when Philip was done, he slowly heaved himself to his feet and said, "Well, I shall do my best to put a stop to all the gossip. I shall let it be known she is a friend of the family whom you have taken under your wing. Meanwhile, shall we repair to the nearest tavern and hoist a pint or two while I tell you the latest on-dits?"

With an impish look that made him seem years younger, Philip agreed. Had he had any notion, any hint, of what Miss Ashbourne was about to do, he would not have been in nearly so good a mood.

Emily stared at the letters on the desk before her and she blinked back tears. Was this truly to be her future? Her father, and a man she could not abide, aiding one another in forcing her to do as they wished?

She could not help but contrast the cold propriety of Mr. Canfield's note with the gentle humor and kindness Mr. Langford had shown her, each day this week when he came to call. Or the little kindnesses he had shown her aunt.

To be sure, she ought not to compare Mr. Langford and

Mr. Canfield. She was betrothed to one while the other saw her as a nuisance he had somehow conceived a responsibility to watch out for, nothing more.

Emily sighed. Her own replies were written and sealed. She would send them off as soon as she had written another letter, this one to the leader of those at the mill who looked to her for hope of change.

She supposed she was fortunate that any of the workers could read. But it meant that they expected some sort of regular reports from her and it was becoming more and more difficult to write them.

For all his promises to help, Mr. Langford had not exaggerated when he said the possibilities were limited. Without consulting him she had written a number of men considered to be sympathetic to the cause of mill workers. And none had been encouraging.

She suspected that if they realized E. Ashbourne was a woman, they would have been even less forthcoming. So what was she to do? Visit these gentlemen in person? She was well aware how frowned upon such a step would be. And yet, was there any other choice?

Even if Mr. Langford was not palming her off with promises he did not mean to keep, ultimately this was her responsibility and she ought to see it carried out herself. She would do what she ought to have done when she first came to London. She would go to see Lord Darton.

Emily set aside her pen and frowned. Why hadn't Sir Thomas Levenger been willing to give her Lord Darton's direction? Why had he sent her to Mr. Langford instead? To be sure, the barrister was very kind, but he was not a member of Parliament as Lord Darton was.

Well, no matter. It was time she made her own decision to do so. Setting aside the one letter left to write, Emily rose to her feet. She would go change her dress, fetch her bonnet, and this time she would ask Whiten to send for a carriage. Even with Lord Darton, she had a shrewd notion that she had best visit without warning. He could not turn her away nearly so easily if she did so.

Emily chose a brown gown made of wool. It was more than a year old, and a trifle out of style, but it contrived to make her—she hoped—look both older and more respectable than she was. If she was going to go against propriety, by calling upon a gentleman, even Lord Darton, then she had best look as respectable as possible.

Emily studied her image in the mirror. She still did not look quite as old or as proper as she wished. Biting her lower lip, she did up her hair in a bun so severe that she resembled her aunt.

Whiten sent for a carriage, betraying not by a flicker of his eyes how improper he thought it was for her to sally forth alone. The coachman was not nearly so polite. When asked to take her to Lord Darton's town house he replied, "One, I don'ts knows where the cove lives and two, gentlemen don'ts likes their fancy pieces calling at the front door."

Mortified, Emily flushed a deep red. She looked hastily about to make certain no one had overheard the coachman's comments, but the street was fortunately deserted and Whiten was back inside the house.

Perhaps she should have tried to discover Lord Darton's precise direction first, but she had not and her impulsiveness had once again pressed her into an awkward situation.

She tilted her chin up and said haughtily, "Very well, if you don't know Lord Darton's direction, then take me to White's. You must know where that is! Lord Darton is a family friend and I shall look for him there."

The coachman looked at her doubtfully and even muttered under his breath, but in the end he did as she asked. Emily had barely settled herself onto the shabby seat of the hired coach when it jolted forward, setting off down the street at a brisk pace.

It was not, Emily knew, the thing for a woman to call at White's. And she did not expect to be admitted, but she had heard that most gentlemen spent much of their days there and surely the doorman would have Lord Darton fetched to speak with her if she asked him to do so.

And if Lord Darton was not at White's, perhaps other members of Parliament would be. Not that they were likely to be pleased to see her, either. Emily knew that pressing her interests at White's was likely to shock the men there. But she had never been one to shirk a task merely because it would not be an easy one.

And surely, if she claimed urgent business and threw herself on the sympathy of the gentlemen there, someone would listen to her? If not a member of Parliament, then at least a gentleman who had the ear of one. And surely they would not look too harshly on her when they understood it was the only way to find the men she needed to speak with? Particularly Lord Darton. If he were there, everything would be easy. This Lord Darton was not the man her uncle had known, but how unlike his father could he be?

Emily Ashbourne was supremely naive.

Two hours later found her in the admitting room of Bedlam.

Chapter 8

Lord Darton, when he stopped to think of it, was rather fond of his three younger brothers, but there was no denying they, each of them, were rather intimidating and showed a distinct lack of respect toward him, as well as a distressing tendency to act in ways most inappropriate for gentlemen. Still, he made it a point to see them regularly, feeling that as head of the family he had a responsibility to keep tabs on what they were about.

Now, Lord Darton might have invited his brothers to his house, and upon occasion he did so. There was no denying, however, that Philip, James, and Harry did not get along particularly well with Athenia, Lady Darton. So, far more often, George arranged to meet one or more of his brothers at his club and dine with them there.

There was always a quiet corner where he could interrogate one or the other of them, if he felt the need, and no fear that Athenia would complain, the next morning, about his brothers' lack of manners and respect toward her.

This was one such evening and George even congratulated himself that for once he would be the one with an astonishing story to tell. His brothers were forever roasting him that he lived a dull life! What would they think when they learned that a madwoman had tried to storm White's today and then accosted him as he was leaving and attempted to tell him the position he ought to take on points of law!

So, in excellent humor, Lord Darton strode into his club,

where he discovered the story had preceded him. Well, a version of the story, at any rate. He was not identified by name. Nor was the woman in question. But since Darton himself had not paid a great deal of attention to that little detail, it was not surprising no one else had.

In any event, since he had not been identified, he would be able to surprise his brothers with that morsel of information. Besides, they were not here yet and perhaps they had heard nothing of the affair, and he would be the first to tell them what had occurred after all.

His first glimpse of them confirmed Darton in his affection for his brothers. Philip had dignity and James was the epitome of a gentleman, elegantly turned out with exquisitely tailored clothes. No one looking at him would ever guess he dabbled in things. If only they both did not have such eccentric interests!

George suppressed a shudder at the thought and stepped forward to greet his brothers. After the usual exchange of pleasantries, they went in to dinner. Darton's experienced eye told him that both James and Philip had already indulged a bit, but that was all to the good. It would take the edge off their wits and grant him a level playing field. It also had patently improved their tempers.

Indeed, so well did they get along, that the first hint of trouble came over the port, after dinner, as George began to relate the story of his day. He had gotten as far as describing the deranged damsel when abruptly Philip rose to his feet, nearly overturning the table.

In accents thick with wine, Philip demanded, "Where did they take her? Where is she now?"

Darton blinked in amazement at his brother. "Why, I don't know," he said. "Bedlam, I must suppose. That's where I told them to take her."

And then, Philip turned on his heel and strode out of the room without another word. George watched him, mouth agape, then turned to James to see what he made of this odd behavior.

"How much did the pair of you have to drink before dinner?" George demanded.

James looked at him and answered carefully, with wide, solemn eyes, "I don't think the problem is how much Philip has had to drink."

"Then what the devil is the problem?" George demanded testily. "Leaving like that! It's downright rude, it is, and so I shall tell Philip the next time I see him. And why the devil was he asking the whereabouts of that girl?"

A mischievous expression crossed James's face, causing Lord Darton to feel distinctly uneasy. Nor was he reassured by his brother's carefully phrased answer.

"I think you recalled to Philip a certain client of his and he has gone to satisfy himself as to her welfare."

"Her welfare?" George echoed. "Do you mean to say some widow is consulting him?"

James only smiled more broadly, and his eyes began to dance. "I think," he said judiciously, "I shall leave it to Philip to answer your questions. If he chooses to do so. As for me, I am pledged to friends for an evening of cards. A perfectly proper occupation for a gentleman, I know you will agree and therefore excuse me."

And before Darton could think of a way to deny it, James was on his feet and leaving the room. George could only stare fixedly at the bottle of port and wonder if madness was catching and, if so, whether London was about to be gripped by an epidemic of it.

Philip was admitted, though not without protest, when he presented himself at the doors of Bedlam a short time later. The director, hastily roused from his bed and summoned to deal with the irascible barrister, was not in a mood to be conciliatory.

"In the morning. Come back in the morning," he told

Philip curtly. "We do not conduct tours at this hour of the night. I cannot understand why anyone thought it necessary to wake me to have me tell you so."

"I do not wish for a tour of Bedlam," Philip answered, holding onto his temper with great effort, "I am looking for a girl."

"Oh. A girl. Well, why didn't you just apply to the guard? For the proper fee—"

In a moment, Philip had the man by the throat. "I am looking for a very specific girl. And not for the purpose you seem to think! This girl is a young lady. And if she has been hurt, in any way, you will regret it. I shall have this place shut down and you clapped up into prison! The girl who was brought in here this afternoon is my ward and I want to see her right now!"

It was a lie, but not entirely. Philip realized that at some point he had come to think of himself as Miss Ashbourne's guardian, albeit not a legal one. But this man was not to know the difference.

The director managed to choke out a reply and Philip let him go. Instantly the man retreated to the far side of the room. He opened the door and sent the guard to fetch the latest charge, as he called her. Then he turned back to Philip.

"Your ward!" he echoed, recovering remarkably quickly. "I wonder, then, that you do not take better care of her. She ought to be kept under lock and key."

Philip did not bother to argue. At the moment, in fact, he was inclined to agree. Once he had Miss Ashbourne safely away from here, he meant to ring a peal over her head that she would never forget! One calculated to ensure she never acted with such foolishness again.

But the thought died the moment he saw her. Philip had heard about Bedlam, though he had never come to laugh at the inmates, as some did. Nor to hire any for an hour or two of pleasure. Such a thing would have been entirely repugnant to him, but he had heard the stories.

Still, when Miss Ashbourne was brought into the room, Philip was completely unprepared for the appalling change in her appearance since last he saw the girl. Her dress was torn in more than one place. Her hair was tangled, with half the pins holding it gone. And her bonnet was missing as well. The look on her face tore at his heart and he wanted to reach out to hold her.

Indeed, he had taken half a step in her direction when suddenly her face snapped up and her eyes lit on him and she smiled.

"Mr. Langford! I did not look for you to come and rescue me! How did you know I was here?"

Philip turned to the director. "Mad?" he demanded. "As you can hear, she is as sane as you or I."

The director began to stammer. "She—she was not so coherent when she was brought in. She was shouting curses and behaving in a most unladylike way! And the guards who brought her, they said she had behaved like a madwoman. Naturally, I took their word for it."

"Naturally," Philip echoed with great irony.

She came farther into the room and stepped between the two men. The guard made as if to stop her but a signal from the director stopped him.

"Mr. Langford, may we go home now? To be sure, there is a great deal that needs investigating in this place, but at the moment I wish nothing more than to be away from here," she said.

Instantly he moved to her side and took her arm. "Of course."

The director did not try to stop them, though his parting words were, "Sometimes they have lucid moments! It doesn't mean they are sane."

Outside, the coachman recoiled at the sight of Miss Ashbourne, for her cloak was long gone and she had nothing to cover her torn dress.

"She ain't violent, guv'nor, is she?" he asked.

"It's all right. Her being here was a mistake. Now corrected," Philip assured the man. "The lady is quite sane, I assure you."

The coachman shook his head. "Taking up ladies, now, is they? A shame, that's what it is, a right shame."

Since Philip was inclined to agree, he tossed the man a coin and helped Miss Ashbourne into the carriage. The sooner they were away from here, the better. For once he was grateful that she lived in as poor a section of London as she did. He shuddered to think what it would do to her reputation if she lived in more respectable parts and were seen in this condition when he took her home.

Inside the carriage, he expected to find a much subdued Miss Ashbourne. He ought to have known better. The moment the carriage door was closed she began to speak.

"We must do something about that place! Conditions are shocking. You would not believe what goes on in there. We must do something about it."

Not a word of pity for herself. Not the least sign of the hysterics which any other lady of his acquaintance would have indulged in. She did not scream with terror, as a proper lady ought to have done. Instead Miss Ashbourne was already demanding that he help her to reform the place.

It was too much to be borne. Philip could not help himself. He snapped at her, "I thought what landed you there was your determination to do something! Did you have to choose to harass Lord Darton?"

She crossed her arms and glared at him. "How was I to know he would be such a pompous fool? Or that he would go so far as to have me carted off to Bedlam?"

Then, a small frown appeared and she said, more temperately, "How did you know it was Lord Darton who did so? Indeed, how did you know I was there at all?"

"It is the talk of London," Philip said scathingly.

Once again she did not react in the least as he expected. Her eyes glowed and she grinned. "Famous!"

He recoiled. He could not help himself. "You are prepared to wed a man you cannot abide, in order to salvage your reputation," he said scathingly, "but you do not object, indeed you are pleased, that all of London thinks you mad? I begin to think Darton had the right of it."

Now an angry look came into her eyes. "You appear to have forgotten that my father threatened to throw me penniless into the street if I did not agree to the match."

Philip flinched. He had forgotten. She apparently noticed the reaction, for she leaned forward and pressed the point.

"Pray tell me how else I am to avoid such a match that is so disagreeable to me than to give my bridegroom-to-be a distaste of me?"

"Are you so certain it will?" Philip asked cautiously. "If the fellow has a *tendre* for you, he may well choose to stand by you, nonetheless. He must, after all, know what you are like."

She laughed and it was not a pretty sound. Indeed, it was harsh in the confines of the carriage and her eyes glittered with so much anger that Philip was even more taken aback than before.

"A *tendre*? Not Canfield! Though he once tried to make me believe it was so. No, Mr. Canfield wishes to rise above his station and he means to do so by marrying well. I had the misfortune to be the only young lady, within the vicinity, who could possibly suit his purposes. But if I am ruined, because I have been proclaimed mad, why then I shall do him no good whatsoever."

Philip's blood ran cold at the appalling picture her words painted in his mind. And, not for the first time, he felt a strong desire to draw this Mr. Canfield's cork.

Still, he was a barrister, and he felt himself compelled to point out the flaws in her plan. He ticked them off on his fingers.

"First of all, the news may not reach your home village,"

he said. "Second, surely those who know you there will know the charge to be false."

She leaned forward. "Will they? I have always been accounted eccentric, this will merely seem one step more. As for ensuring the news reaches home, why, I shall gently encourage Aunt Agatha to write Papa, and some of her friends there, in the strictest confidence, of course, of her dismay at my odd behavior and the disastrous consequences it brought down upon my head."

He nodded. She appeared to have thought of a great many answers. Still there was one more point to consider. Gently he said, "But have you considered? What if you do wish to marry, someday? You have effectively ruined yourself not only in the eyes of Mr. Canfield but in the eyes of any other possible suitor."

One tiny tear trickled down her cheek and it wrung his heart. But there was dignity in her voice and a refusal to accept his pity as she said quietly, "You have said yourself, sir, that you could well understand why I have not found a husband by the age of three and twenty. It has long been apparent to me that I am unlikely ever to do so, whether I ruined myself as I did tonight or not."

He felt the oddest impulse to take Miss Ashbourne in his arms and comfort her. Fortunately, sufficient common sense remained that he did not. Instead he inclined his head stiffly, indicating the truth of what she said.

But it wasn't true, a tiny voice whispered at the back of Philip's mind. Even in her torn gown and with her hair tumbling all about her shoulders, Miss Ashbourne was oddly appealing. And he found himself wondering what it would be like to kiss her. What it would be like to come home to her, to a woman who could actually talk to him about things that mattered.

Yes, odd was definitely the correct word here. Miss Ashbourne was an odd duckling and one few men would stop to consider for a bride. It took Philip aback to realize he had even thought the word and he made haste to focus on all the legal matters that were on his desk, matters that required his attention more than the young woman in the carriage. She was turning his world upside down and that was the last thing he would wish for, wasn't it?

She tried to make it easy for him. She turned her head and pretended to study the window of the carriage. Which would have been a far more effective tactic had he not already drawn the curtains for greater privacy.

As it was, it only made her seem younger, more vulnerable than before. With a muttered curse, Philip said, "What will you do next? Surely this had proven to you that you cannot effect the changes you wish to effect?"

She met his gaze squarely. "I shall not give up, though perhaps," she added reflectively, "I shall not attempt to force my way into White's again. Nor accost gentlemen as they are leaving. I knew it would not be considered proper but I had no notion just how strongly gentlemen would feel about my doing so."

"You ought to have known!"

She did not deny it, only bent her head a little lower. Philip silently cursed. Then, aloud he asked the question which had been troubling him ever since George told him the story.

"Why did you choose Lord Darton to approach? Surely you did not think he would help you?"

"Why not?" she asked indignantly. "His father was a good friend to my uncle. My uncle used to say there was no gentleman in England he would trust more than Lord Darton. That he was one of the few men in England who truly believed in reform."

"This Lord Darton is not like his father, in that respect," Philip replied tightly.

"Yes, so I discovered," Miss Ashbourne said sadly, gazing down into her lap. Then she lifted her eyes to look at him. "But I cannot understand it," she said. "How could Lord

Darton not wish to follow in his father's footsteps? How could he not admire and wish to be like him?"

"Perhaps he saw the effects of being ostracized by all those around his father and chose to not suffer the same," Philip said tightly.

Now she had fire in her eyes. "How cowardly! If I were Lord Darton I should proudly emulate my father! I should not care what anyone else thought, so long as I knew that I was doing what was right! Would you not do the same, Mr. Langford?"

Fortunately she did not wait for an answer since Philip was at a loss to know what he could say. Instead, her forehead furrowed and she frowned as she asked, "In any event, I shall know in the future not to waste my time with Lord Darton. Who should I approach next?"

She was serious. Completely serious. His jaw dropped, then, furious, he thundered, "No one! You should approach no one, Miss Ashbourne. Haven't you learned anything from this debacle?"

"Well, you needn't shout," she said indignantly. "And whatever the difficulties, I must approach someone. What else am I to do?"

He glowered at her. "Go. Home," he suggested, biting off the words.

For a moment she didn't answer. Then another tear trickled down her cheek. Shaken, Philip started to reach out a hand to her but she pulled away.

"Forgive me, Mr. Langford," she said with stiff politeness. "This is not your concern and I keep forgetting that. You have no reason to feel as passionately as I do that the law ought to be changed."

"It is my concern when I am called upon to rescue you," Philip said through clenched teeth.

"No one asked you to do so!" she said hotly.

"And if I had not?" he countered. "Who would have done so?"

Now she flushed and lowered her eyes and bit her lower lip in a gesture Philip found oddly endearing. He wanted more than ever to hold and comfort her. And because the notion frightened him, he looked away.

"You cannot simply accost men as you did today," Philip said, trying to keep his voice gentle.

Miss Ashbourne nodded, but Philip was not deceived into believing she had surrendered. Nor was he mistaken.

"I will not give up," she warned him.

Philip sighed. "At least give me a few days to think of what you might do," he said. "Just a few days without landing yourself in the briars? Or Bedlam again?"

She hesitated but, in the end, nodded her reluctant agreement. "A few days," she echoed.

And then she smiled, truly smiled at Philip. As though she trusted him. As though she believed he would think of a way for her to succeed. As though he were not just like George in having turned his back on their father and all that the late Lord Darton had believed in.

Philip sighed to himself and wondered what madness he had gotten himself into now!

Chapter 9

It was too much to hope that the incident would not be talked about. The only fortunate circumstance, in Philip's opinion, was that no one seemed to know who the woman was. Or that she was a lady.

George, Lord Darton, had supposed her to be a deranged maidservant who had somehow gotten hold of her mistress's clothing. Someone, not close enough to overhear, had presumed her to be a cast-off mistress who wished to tax Lord Darton with the unfortunate results of his liaison with her.

This was the source of much amusement among those who knew Lord Darton well, for he was accounted a rigidly proper fellow who had probably never had a mistress in his life. But nonetheless few could resist the urge to repeat the jest and roast him for it.

Fortunately for Miss Ashbourne's reputation, no one seemed to know the name of the supposed temptress and her description grew more lurid with each telling until it was most unlikely anyone would recognize the woman who inspired it.

Philip shuddered at the thought of having to tell his brother the truth about Miss Ashbourne and his own connection with her. He decided, with some justice, that there was no point in even attempting to do so. With luck, the two would never meet again and he need never try.

When he called upon Miss Jarrod and Miss Ashbourne, he was not certain whether to be relieved or distressed that the elder lady had responded precisely as the younger one had predicted. He discovered that it nettled him to know Miss Ashbourne appeared to have more control over her relatives than he had over his.

"I must thank you for rescuing Emily," Miss Jarrod told Philip, grasping his hand fervently between hers. "I do wish you had allowed me to say so last night! But you rushed off before I had a chance to do so."

She paused and Philip drew breath to answer her. But before he could, she had released his hand and turned to Miss Ashbourne.

"I don't know what your father is going to say," Miss Jarrod told her niece tearfully. "I know he is going to blame me. But how could I stop you? I had no notion what you planned."

She whirled back to face Philip again, leaving him feeling a trifle dizzy.

"I did have to write her father, didn't I, Mr. Langford? He does have a right to know, doesn't he? I did also write the vicar's wife and ask her to try to calm Emily's father, but I fear it is a hopeless cause. We may expect, any day, to have him posting down here to take us back or a letter summoning us home."

One glance at Miss Ashbourne assured Philip that she seemed no worse for wear. She also appeared quite content to let her aunt rant and rave. And well she should, since the poor woman had done precisely what Miss Ashbourne wished her to do!

Finally Miss Jarrod wound down and suddenly she smiled, a gleam in her eye as mischievous as any he had seen before. "The only good thing," she said shrewdly, "is that now Mr. Canfield will not force my niece to marry him. And that may be worth all the trouble Emily has caused.

She seemed to expect Philip to answer but he merely bowed. Let her take it as she wished. He was not about to become drawn into that discussion!

Still, Miss Jarrod was apparently satisfied. She settled into the nearest chair and said to Emily, "I presume we have less than a fortnight left in London, my dear. What do you mean to do with the time you have left?"

Miss Ashbourne grinned at her aunt, completely unrepentantly. "Get into more trouble," she said.

Far from appearing to be dismayed or overcome with the vapors, Miss Jarrod nodded approvingly. Philip, however, was moved to protest.

"Surely, Miss Jarrod, you do not countenance such foolishness? You said you would have tried to stop her if you knew what your niece intended."

"On the contrary," Miss Jarrod replied placidly, "I would have felt I ought to stop her. That is another matter entirely. And precisely why I have advised Emily to tell me as little as possible about her plans. Then I can quite honestly tell her father I knew nothing beforehand."

"But you know she means to get into more trouble," Philip pointed out acidly.

"But not what sort, or how," Miss Jarrod shot back. "And I don't mean to know," she added hastily, before Philip could tell her.

Abruptly she lost her somewhat vacant air and stared fixedly at the barrister. "I trust my niece, Mr. Langford, to do what is right. Not what is conventional or proper or what her father would approve, but what is right."

"You must know," Miss Ashbourne added lightly, "that my aunt, despite her conventional appearance, has always encouraged me to read the most astonishing things. Whether she wishes to acknowledge it or not, it is due to her guidance that I hold the views that I do."

Philip gaped at both of them. There was, there could be, he thought, no answer to that. Now he fixed his attention on Miss Ashbourne. He stared at her grimly. She, however, did not seem in the least discomposed.

Dressed today in an elegant morning gown, in a becoming shade of blue, with her hair dressed in a topknot and curls, it was hard to believe this was the same woman he had rescued from Bedlam the night before. Suddenly it was too much for Philip's temper.

"Do you have any notion what could have happened to you in Bedlam?" he demanded. "Any notion what the guards are said to do to their female inmates? Or what they will allow others to do, if paid to look the other way?"

Her gaze did not waver in the slightest, though the look in her eyes also turned grim.

"I am not a fool, Mr. Langford. It took me all of five minutes inside that place to guess." Her voice quavered slightly, and Miss Ashbourne paused to draw a deep, steadying breath. Then she went on. "And I do not intend to go back there ever again. At least not," she added with an alarming hint of mischief in her eyes, "as an inmate."

Philip threw up his hands. What was he to do with such a person? And yet he had to try to make her see reason, however impossible the task.

"You do not intend to go back," he echoed sardonically, "yet you plan to cause trouble. Well, Miss Ashbourne, if you do cause trouble, the odds are very great that someone else will get sufficiently exasperated to try to send you back there again. Have you not thought of that?"

She did not answer at once. And when she did speak, it was to Miss Jarrod. "Perhaps, Aunt Agatha," she said, "you ought to leave us alone for a few minutes. I do not think you wish to know what I mean to say to Mr. Langford."

Miss Jarrod hesitated. She wrinkled her nose. "It would be most improper," she said. She turned to look at Philip and said brightly, "I don't suppose you have your carriage with you? For then you could take Emily for a drive around one of the parks and that would be unexceptionable."

"I walked," Philip said shortly.

Miss Jarrod appeared to think. "The garden," she suggested. A moment later she added doubtfully, "At least, I think it is supposed to be a garden, even though it has only a few very straggly, unfortunate plants left in it. Still, you could take a turn about the garden with my niece. That would be all right."

The older woman smiled triumphantly, as though delighted to have thought of a solution. Miss Ashbourne was already rising to her feet and Philip did so as well, almost without thinking. To Miss Jarrod he said in acid tones, "You have a most convenient conscience, ma'am."

But she was undaunted. "I do, don't I?" she agreed. "And why my brother-in-law was so foolish as to believe otherwise is beyond me."

Now Miss Ashbourne laughed. "Papa had no choice. There was no one else he could send with me to London," she pointed out. "Besides, at home you keep a much closer eye on me than you have done here. Now come, Mr. Langford. We are wasting time while you abuse my poor aunt. Come outside to the garden and abuse me, instead, if you must."

But he didn't want to abuse her. He wanted, Philip discovered as he walked behind Miss Ashbourne through the narrow hallway, to take her in his arms. He wanted to pull the pins from her hair and see it tumbled down around her shoulders all over again. And the thought appalled him!

He had, in some sort, taken Miss Ashbourne into his care. He owed her civility and the best advice he could give her and rigid propriety. Not to have him thinking of her as if she was some sort of wanton creature.

But he didn't. He didn't think of her as wanton, he realized with a shock. He wanted to imagine her letting down her hair only for him. And he wanted as much to continue to protect her as to draw her to him for a kiss.

Of course he did nothing of the sort. Instead, bewildered by his own thoughts, Philip allowed Miss Ashbourne to put an extra pace or two between them. And he kept his face impassive as she led him through the kitchen to get to the back garden. The thing was, as Miss Jarrod had said, scarcely worthy of the name, but it was undeniable that here, at least, they had some privacy.

And however reprehensible it might be, Philip found he was unaccountably glad of that. Behind the brick walls that enclosed this small space, they were alone and it was possible to forget, or at least pretend to forget, all the dictates societies would impose upon them.

"What is it you wished to tell me?" he asked Miss Ashbourne.

She tilted her head. "Have you thought of anything yet? Anything I can do?"

Philip hesitated. He chose his words carefully. "What do you hope to accomplish?" he asked. "You will not change men's minds. Not by yourself and not even with me beside you. Indeed, if we try, we may both find ourselves clapped up into Bedlam!"

She met his gaze unflinchingly. "It will not come to that," she said quietly. "I do not mean to make, again, the sort of mistake I made yesterday. And while I know you think me a fool, I do not expect to truly change anyone's mind. Yesterday, I still believed it was possible for me to do so, all by myself. Today, I am wiser."

She paused and took a deep breath, and he could see what the effort cost her. "I shan't change their minds, but perhaps, indeed I hope, I shall at least begin to make these men think. Perhaps I can prick at their consciences so that, in time, when others speak to them, they may remember what I said, as well. In any event, whether I can succeed or not, I must try."

Philip did not like to be cruel but he could see no alternative save to tell her the truth. "They will not believe you because you are a woman," he said bluntly.

"You are a man," she countered.

"But I have not seen these conditions."

She smiled. And the moment she smiled, Philip knew he

had made an error. A grave error. He took a step backward. She took a step toward him. "You could come and see for yourself," she said coaxingly.

Philip felt even greater alarm than before. He stopped backing up and put his hands on her arms. "Listen to me, Miss Ashbourne," he said firmly. "I have far too much to do here, in London, to go rushing off to look at mills and factories and such. Whatever the cause."

She regarded him steadily for a moment, searching his eyes. Apparently what she saw convinced her, for her shoulders slumped in defeat.

He could not bear it. There must be something he could say to take away the look on her face. And then he knew what to offer, what hope that would not require him to dash all over the countryside. He turned the idea over and over in his head and could see no flaw in his plan. It would even keep her out of trouble. He hoped. He smiled.

Emily did not trust Mr. Langford's smile. It betokened a sense of triumph she did not like to see. Not when she knew he had been so outspoken in his belief that what she intended was futile. She did not think she was going to like what he was about to say.

His words confirmed her fears.

"My dear Miss Ashbourne, if you wish to influence these gentlemen, you would have far more success if you attempted to do so on the dance floor than by storming White's where they cannot help but think you an intruder."

Emily held on to her temper with great effort. "And suppose I am recognized?"

He hesitated only a moment. "I think it most unlikely," he said smoothly. "The description of you circulating about London bears little resemblance to the reality. And if someone thinks they recognize you, you need merely stare them out of countenance. Besides, by the time you have been presented at court—"

"I have been," she said, cutting him short. At his look of surprise she added unwillingly, "I was brought to London for a Season when I was seventeen. I disliked it intensely and managed to land myself in the briars within a few weeks and found myself back home rusticating, where I assure you I much preferred to be."

"I see."

Emily sighed. "No, you don't. Your suggestion might have some merit," she said evenly, "if there were some way, any way, for me to procure invitations to balls and routs and parties and such. But even I am not such a want-wit as to suppose the patronesses of Almack's are likely to grant me the entrée, particularly after the manner in which I left London six years ago. And without invitations, your notion will come to naught."

"That," he countered, "is your dilemma. I have offered you what I believe to be the only possible way to proceed. If you choose not to follow my advice . . ."

He had the audacity to shrug as he allowed his voice to trail off. It was a challenge, deliberately offered, and Emily had never drawn back from a challenge in her life.

Perhaps, she thought with a hint of despair, she ought to marry Mr. Canfield, after all. As his wife, she might be able to effect changes in his mills more easily than she could persuade the lords here in London.

A moment's reflection, however, sufficed to make her realize that no one could alter Mr. Canfield's methods. More than one overseer had attempted to do so and everyone knew of the public and immediate dismissal each had faced. No, she would have to try to prevail here, in London, however difficult and frustrating a task it might be.

Besides, Mr. Langford was looking at her with a smug expression on his face, certain he had spiked her guns, and it would give her great pleasure to do what he obviously believed to be impossible for her.

Emily straightened her shoulders without even realizing

she did so. Her chin came up and her eyes sparkled in the most alarming way.

"Suppose I do as you suggest," she said. "Contrive a way to appear on the dance floor with these gentlemen. Will you be by my side to help persuade them?"

If she had hoped to disconcert Mr. Langford, she was mistaken. To be sure, there had been a moment when he started, his eyes widened, and he seemed about to object. But it was only a moment, a very brief one, and then he, too, straightened.

Mr. Langford bowed gallantly. "My dear Miss Ashbourne, if you meet these men on the dance floor, you will not have the slightest need of my help. Your beauty alone will charm them into doing what you wish."

Emily said a rude word. It was a word much in favor in the stable yard among the grooms back home. It patently took Mr. Langford aback. She followed it with another. Then she sighed.

"Mr. Langford," she said with exaggerated patience, "if you wish to renege on your promise, that is one thing. But do not, I pray you, insult me with meaningless nonsense not even a baby could pretend to believe. You wish to set me a task you believe impossible. Then you can say that you would have stood by my side, but I failed on my part of the bargain. Well, Mr. Langford, I shall not fail. And then you, sir, will find that you must either prove a false witness or do as you have said you would."

Emily was in a towering rage. She had wanted, so dearly, to believe in Mr. Langford and his promise. She had wanted to believe that here, at last, was someone who would act as her champion.

Well, she ought to have known better! she told herself, even as she turned her back on him and dashed a tear from her eye. She would not let him see how overset she was. She would not let him guess how much she had counted on his support!

Over her shoulder she said, "I am certain you can find your way out by yourself, Mr. Langford. My aunt will understand your precipitous departure. Good day, sir. I shall not trouble you again.

But before she had taken more than two steps, Emily felt a pair of hands grasp her shoulders. She half expected him to spin her around to face him, but he did not do so. Instead his hands squeezed tight, repeatedly, and she held her breath to hear what he would say.

His voice, when it came, was so low she had to strain to hear it. "You mistake me, Miss Ashbourne. I do believe this is the best way for you to proceed. And I promise that when you find a way to attend a ball or party, I shall come as well and stand by you."

Now she pulled free and turned to face him, a puzzled look on her face. "But what if you don't have an invitation?" she asked.

He gave her a cynical smile, one so cold it made Emily flinch.

"Oh, never fear," he said with a bitter edge to his voice, "I am a presentable, unmarried man. I may only be a barrister, but I do have a snug little estate, as well as a London town house, left me by an uncle, along with sufficient funds to support it. I have never, until perhaps now, engaged in any behavior likely to cover me with scandal. You may trust me when I say that no hostess will turn me away."

Emily swallowed hard. So he thought she would bring scandal down upon his head? The worst of it was, he was probably right. Still, she could only nod, for this was too important for her to refuse his help. She hoped it would not end with Mr. Langford hating her, but if it accomplished her goals, she would do it in a shot.

So, aloud, she said, "Thank you, Mr. Langford. I shall hold you to that promise. And now, good day."

And if he bowed and left with alacrity, what was there to

upset her in that? She had what she wanted, didn't she? She had his promise to help her.

But there was a part of her that hoped, desperately, he would not come to hate her in the end, after all.

Chapter 10

James was, as Philip rather expected, waiting for him at his London town house when he returned that evening. It had been too much to hope that James would not have realized who the lady must be that George had had carted off to Bedlam. Thank heavens he could be trusted to hold his tongue! Still, Philip was less than pleased to see him.

"Don't you have some engagement tonight?" Philip demanded irritably. "Cards or dancing or something?"

James, the absolute picture of a dandy, regarded his neatly buffed nails, then smiled and shook his head. "No," he said sweetly.

Philip gritted his teeth and offered his brother some brandy. In answer, James held up a half-full glass and said, "Thank you but your valet—an excellent fellow, by the way, I may steal him from you one of these days—has already seen to the matter."

"Very well, then, out with it! What do you want?"

James raised his eyebrows and pretended to look offended, but Philip knew him too well for that to wash. His younger brother was laughing at him. Which he could have borne with equanimity, save that he could read concern in James's eyes as well.

When Philip did not answer, his brother became even more blunt.

"Did you rescue the fair damsel last night?" James asked.

"I presume it was your fair damsel George was talking about?"

"It was and I did."

James raised his eyebrows even more at this curt tone. "Was it too late?" he asked, all teasing gone from his voice now.

Philip shook his head. "Not in the way you mean. But I fear her reputation will be fairly destroyed should anyone ever learn about her adventure."

"Hers or George's," James countered, the mischief back in his eyes. "Just think, our brother George, the epitome of propriety, tossing a lady into Bedlam!"

Against his will, Philip began to grin at the image. For James was right—George would be mortified to learn what he had done. To send a maidservant to Bedlam was a right and proper thing to do, in his mind. But a lady? Never!

James grinned as well. "Shall I tell him?" he asked, his eyes twinkling at the thought.

At once the amusement left Philip's eyes. "No!"

At James's look of surprise, Philip reluctantly went on, "It will only harm Miss Ashbourne's reputation, even for George to know. Time enough if he encounters her on the dance floor. Though I do not think it will come to that. Still, she did seem determined."

"What the devil are you muttering about?" James demanded impatiently. "Meet George on the dance floor? Yesterday you said the girl had no intention, or means, of getting caught up in the Season."

Philip hesitated, then sighed. He had already said too much. He had best tell his brother the whole of it, for James would never let it be. And James, even more than he, had the power to help Miss Ashbourne, if he chose. The trouble was, Philip thought, he didn't know if he wanted her helped. Still, he decided to tell James the plan he had suggested to Miss Ashbourne.

When he was done, his brother was silent for several mo-

ments. Then James nodded to himself. "I know a lady or two
to speak to. Sally Jersey, for one. And if she takes the girl
under her wing, that should do the trick. Mind," he said,
holding up a finger, "she must not count on vouchers for Almack's. That is beyond even my realm of ability to procure.
But invitations for a few balls and such, yes, that much I
think I can do."

Philip did not know whether to be pleased or alarmed.
Hastily deciding, he said, "I shouldn't wish to put you to any
trouble. And Miss Ashbourne did say she that had retired
from London in disgrace a few years ago. So it may not be
possible."

James smiled in a way that his older brother profoundly
mistrusted. His next few words confirmed Philip's worst
fears.

"Oh, I think there may be a way. The *ton* has a conve-
niently short memory when it suits. And I assure you that it
is no trouble to me. I should enjoy helping this Miss Ashbourne. Any young lady who can twist my brother around
her finger, as she appears to have done, is definitely worthy
of any help I can give her. Trouble? Oh, no, dear brother, it
will be, I assure you, a great, great pleasure to assist Miss
Ashbourne."

Philip opened his mouth to object, to say that she had not
wrapped him around her finger. And then he closed his
mouth again. Somehow he had the sinking notion that anything he said would only get him into a deeper morass than
before.

"Thank you," he said, letting the irony show in his voice.
"I am all gratitude for your generous assistance."

But James was undaunted. Even as he rose to his feet he
grinned unrepentantly and said, "No, you're not. Not yet,
anyway. But, unless I've greatly misjudged this Miss Ashbourne—which is possible since I've never met her—sooner
or later you will be. No, no, don't trouble to thank me. Or to
show me out. No doubt you've some boring books you wish

to pore over, or some such thing, and I've an engagement I'm already late for."

And then he was gone. Philip could only feel a profound sense of relief. He loved his brother, but were he ever to get through a week without wishing to strangle him at least once, he would count it something of a miracle. And this week was clearly no exception.

With a sigh, Philip rang for a servant and gave orders for his dinner to be served in an hour, and then, just as James had predicted, reached for one of the law books he kept at home. It was, his friends and even his brothers thought, a shocking circumstance.

It was bad enough, they told him, that he had decided to take up the law and become a barrister. That was eccentric enough. But to be serious about it! To actually intend to work at the profession? That was what they found all but unforgivable.

A pity. Because studying and practicing the law was what Philip intended to do, for the rest of his life. It was, quite simply, what he loved.

Unfortunately for his peace of mind, Philip thought to look at his mail. There was a letter from Harry, which he reached for first.

It ought to have set his mind at rest to know that Harry, at least when this was written, was unhurt. But it was a most distressing letter.

My dear brother, Harry wrote, *news will soon reach London of the fighting here. It was, and continues to be, fierce, with many casualties to our side. The enemy was too well informed and I suspect treachery. Please discover what you can about a man, a mill owner, named Richard Canfield, but do not commit anything to paper. I shall come for the information myself, when I can. Yours, Harry.*

It was such a typical letter, Philip thought. He set it carefully in the locked drawer of the desk, knowing Harry would not want prying eyes to see it. He should burn it, but not until he had read it several times through. Richard Canfield. The name struck him like a chill. Surely it could not be the same man Miss Ashbourne had mentioned? That would be far too much of a coincidence. And yet, perhaps it was. Stranger things had been known to happen. Sir Thomas had said the man owned a mill.

Philip wished his brother was here to ask him all the questions that came to mind. But as it was, he would do his best to fulfill Harry's request. And hope that Harry came to claim his information soon.

Emily was having no easier a time of it. Aunt Agatha was regarding her as if she had lost her wits.

"Parties? You wish to go to parties?"

"Yes, Aunt Agatha."

Miss Jarrod leaned closer. "You never said anything of this before," she said suspiciously.

Emily opened her eyes wide and tried to look innocent. She didn't succeed very well. "But, Aunt Agatha, when I came in from the garden you were nowhere to be found."

Miss Jarrod blinked, then smiled, then said triumphantly, "Oh, the garden! Then this is because of Mr. Langford? Why, that's different, Emily. Of course, if you wish to have a respectable way to see him again, I shall help you! I said I liked Mr. Langford. I like him much better than I like Mr. Canfield. Indeed, I think it a great pity you ever agreed to marry the man! Though I do understand why you did so. Still, this shall answer much better. Much better indeed."

Helplessly, Emily tried to interrupt the woman. "No, Aunt Agatha! It is not that way at all! It is all part of my plan!"

The change in Miss Jarrod's expression was ludicrous. Emily almost thought she was going to cry.

"Not to see Mr. Langford?" she asked. "It's all part of your plan? Oh, dear."

Emily cast about for a way to persuade her aunt to somehow regain her enthusiasm for the notion. A way that did not include pairing her with Mr. Langford in her aunt's mind. But it was too late. Miss Jarrod was smiling again.

"Well, I suppose, whatever your motives, it will still throw you into his company. And that of other men like him. And your father could scarcely disapprove," she said. "Very well, Emily, I shall see what I can do. It has been some time, but some of my dearest girlhood friends are here in London. I could call on one or two and see if they will help you and invite you to their parties."

Emily breathed a sigh of relief. Unfortunately, her relief was a trifle premature, for now Aunt Agatha turned a stern gaze on her and said, "New clothes. You will order new clothes. And at least three new ball gowns or I shan't lift a finger to help you."

She wanted to argue, she wanted to protest that it would be a foolish expenditure. But Emily had known her aunt all her life and while Miss Jarrod was generally accounted to be the mildest and sweetest of creatures, easily bullied, there was a look that sometimes appeared and when it did, her mind was made up. When it was, nothing and no one had ever been known to sway it.

That look was in her eyes right now. Besides, Emily had to acknowledge that if one were going into battle, one ought to marshal the best resources and weapons possible. And if Mr. Langford were right, that meant new clothes.

So, with another sigh, Emily said, "Yes, Aunt Agatha. The very first thing tomorrow morning, I shall go and order some new gowns."

"Including three new ball gowns," he aunt reminded her sternly.

"Including three ball gowns," Emily agreed.

"Good girl! I knew you could be sensible," Miss Jarrod said, beaming her approval. "And I shall make some morning calls."

She paused, cast a shrewd eye at her niece, and said, "I know you are silently cursing me, Emily, but really it will answer very well, you know. When your father arrives from the country, he will see that you are immersed in the Season and cannot be expected to simply draw away. You will have all the time you need for your plans here in London. And he will not have the least excuse to blame me since I will be able to prove to him that I have reclaimed your reputation after all!"

Suddenly Agatha realized what she was saying and stopped. She and Emily looked at one another aghast. Slowly, carefully, Emily said, "I hadn't thought of that. It will mean that, won't it? Then what will I do? Mr. Canfield will insist on marrying me, after all!"

Miss Jarrod settled her eyeglasses more firmly on her nose and said, a grim expression on her face, "We shall think of something. I shall not allow that man to marry you, Emily. I disliked him before but now that I have seen Mr. Langford why, I know it to be impossible! Just give me some time, Emily, and we shall think of something."

Privately Emily strongly suspected she would have to think of something all on her own. But she would not, for the world, hurt her aunt by saying so aloud. Instead she went over, bent and kissed Miss Jarrod's cheek, and said soothingly, "Well, we can worry about it later. Perhaps I shall manage to ruin myself all over again and then we shall have the very best of both worlds."

Emily would have drawn away but Miss Jarrod caught her hand. There was a troubled look in her eyes as she said, "Yes, but Emily, your father was ready to throw you out in the street. And no doubt me as well, for not compelling you to do as he wished, if you refused to marry Mr. Canfield. Why are you so certain that he will not throw you out if you ruin yourself some other way?"

Emily did not try to hide the bleak expression in her eyes as she answered, "I am certain of nothing, Aunt Agatha, except that I cannot marry Mr. Canfield. Papa's threat compelled me then, it would not compel me today. Still, it is the thought of what he would do to you that stops me from simply crying off. Surely there must be something I can do which will satisfy Papa and yet leave me free to do as I wish. All we need to do is think of it."

"Is that all we need to do?" Miss Jarrod retorted tartly. "Why then you have relieved my fears completely."

Emily grinned. "No, I haven't. But I will, you'll see."

The trouble was, Miss Jarrod thought, later, as she undressed for bed, Emily meant it. And that worried Miss Jarrod. For when Emily meant well, the whole world had best watch out.

Chapter 11

Matters did not progress quite as swiftly as either Emily or Miss Jarrod or James would have liked. It is no easy thing to achieve an entrée into Society after one has all but ruined oneself. Particularly when one would have been on the fringes in any event.

But Emily and James and Miss Jarrod were determined. As for Philip, he felt a certain sense of relief. So long as Miss Ashbourne turned her energies to trying to receive invitations to social events, he need not worry that she would accost any other gentlemen in the streets again, as she had his older brother.

The longer that took, the better. For once Miss Ashbourne began to receive such invitations, she would expect him to keep his side of the bargain and Philip all but shuddered at the thought of it. He could imagine too well Miss Ashbourne dancing with some peer and then backing him against the wall to insist he support her causes. And expect Philip to stand by her side as she did so!

No, he hoped it would be some time before she and her aunt and his brother succeeded in drawing her into the Season. And it gave him time to ask questions about this Richard Canfield that Harry had asked about. There seemed little doubt that he was indeed the same man as Miss Ashbourne's fiancé. One of the contracts he held was to provide uniforms for the army in Spain.

So Philip was grateful for the extra time. Still, he did not say so aloud. Not to Miss Ashbourne, not to Miss Jarrod, and certainly not to James. He called frequently upon the two ladies and gave all the appearance of being sympathetic to the difficulties they were facing.

It was, in his opinion, going remarkably well. Until the day he arrived to discover a traveling coach in front of Miss Ashbourne's lodgings. An older man was standing on the pavement, cursing a servant.

As Philip watched, the carriage disgorged a younger man, only a few years older than he was. This second man stalked over to the first man and said, "What the devil is the matter, Ashbourne?"

"Blasted fellow has lost my baggage!" he thundered.

"It must have been taken at one of the stops," the servant protested.

"Or forgotten to strap it on, in the first, more likely," the second man said with a shrug.

"I did strap it on, right securely, I did," the servant protested.

"Well it's your fault it's gone!" Mr. Ashbourne retorted. "And you'll be the one running about London, replacing everything! You'd best get started at once. Here, take these funds and mind you bring back what you don't spend! And you"—he turned to the coachman—"find the nearest stables and wait for me to send word as to when you will be needed again."

Then, as the poor servants gaped at their master, Ashbourne and the other man turned their backs on the carriage and went up to the door of the house.

Philip was torn. He wished to go inside as well, but the servant, left behind, looked utterly dismayed by the task before him. To the coachman he said, "How's I supposed to do what he said? I don't know London! How's I supposed to know where to go? What to buy?"

Philip sighed, turned away from the door, and walked over to the servant. Kindly he said, "If you like, I can give you directions as to where you can find what you need for your master."

The fellow gaped at him, then said fervently, "I should be right grateful if you would, sir."

"And I'll drive you," the coachman said. "He won't be needing me for a bit. And if he does, why, it'll be just too bad! He never told me so and how was I to know? Or I'll say he sent around to the wrong stable. I might disremember to send word to tell him where we are until I feels like letting him know. Come, we'll have this done, thanks to this gentleman, before you knows it. And, sir, if you could recommend a good stable, I'd be much obliged."

So Philip found himself doing just that. And by the time he rapped at the front door, waiting until the carriage was down the street before he did so, a fair amount of time had passed.

Whiten showed him promptly into the parlor, but not before Philip had a chance to ask him about the two men. There were definite advantages to having a servant one knew in someone else's household.

"A Mr. Ashbourne, sir. Miss Ashbourne's father, I collect. And a Mr. Canfield. The ladies do not seem best pleased to see them, sir."

The second name caused Philip to clench his fists. But he kept his voice calm as he replied, "Indeed? Then you had best show me in at once. I have been wanting to make the acquaintance of both these gentlemen and now it seems I shall finally have my wish."

Whiten gave him a doubtful look, but did as he was bid.

The moment he stepped into the parlor and saw Miss Ashbourne's pale, distressed expression, Philip was glad he had delayed no longer.

Mr. Ashbourne stared at him, as though affronted by the intrusion. Miss Jarrod silently begged him for help with her eyes. Mr. Canfield, however, at once demanded, "Who

the devil are you and why are you calling upon my fi-
ancée?"

Philip considered and discarded a number of possible answers, all of which would have prudently soothed the man
and his temper. He glanced at Miss Ashbourne and now she,
too, seemed to be begging for his help.

"Mr. Langford is a barrister," Miss Jarrod said timidly,
when the silence drew on too long for her comfort.

That raised eyebrows even more. And again Philip was
tempted to give some calming answer. But then Mr. Ashbourne spoke and it was he who decided the matter.

He rose to his feet, frowned at Philip, and said, "A barrister? Can't abide the profession. All scoundrels, the lot of
you! And not two farthings to rub together unless you become a judge."

It appealed to the worst in Philip's nature. A side of himself he had thought tamed. It seemed he was mistaken, for
now a glint of anger glittered in his eyes as he said, in a cool,
disdainful voice, "Having had a hand in Miss Ashbourne's
ruin, I thought it only right to come and check, from time to
time, on how she is getting along."

Gasps of indrawn breath were, for a very long moment,
the only sound in the room. Then suddenly there was an uproar as everyone spoke at once.

"Mr. Langford!"

"Good God!"

"Sir, you will explain to me what you mean. At once!"

But the only words Philip cared about were Miss Ashbourne's. She glared at him and all but stamped her foot as
she demanded, "How dare you tell such a lie?"

By now her father was mopping his brow and looking
from Philip to Mr. Canfield. The latter gentleman sat very
quietly, looking from Miss Ashbourne to Philip and back.

"I think you had best explain yourself," Canfield said,
echoing Mr. Ashbourne.

Philip shrugged. "I thought you would know precisely

what I mean since I understand you attempted to ruin her as
well."

Another man, were he a gentleman, would have called
Philip out. But Mr. Canfield was not a gentleman and even
if he had been, he would not have been likely to risk his
neck over a mere woman.

It was, to the surprise of everyone, Miss Jarrod who broke
the tension in the room. In her slightly quavering voice she
said, "I wrote you about the incident, Jonathan. Someone
had poor Emily clapped up into Bedlam and Mr. Langford
brought her home from there."

Ashbourne stared at Philip. "Is that what you meant?" he
demanded. "Why the devil didn't you say so, instead of im-
plying something far worse?"

Philip shrugged and didn't even try to answer. Meanwhile, Canfield was frowning. "Precisely how many people know about this debacle?" he asked. "And who are
they?"

Miss Jarrod waved her hands helplessly. "I don't remember who I wrote to, after the event. I daresay three or four of
my closest friends back home."

"And here in London, any number of people know
about it," Miss Ashbourne added helpfully. "I collect that
the members of White's who were present thought it a
great story to tell. Why, we have been trying, for the past
week or more to gain the entrée into Society and been re-
buffed at every turn. Perhaps because the tale is so well
known?"

"You needn't sound as if you were bragging about it!" her
father snapped.

Canfield was calmer. He smiled at Miss Ashbourne and
it was not a pleasant smile. "I told you, I won't believe
such an obvious fabrication. No gentleman would throw a
lady into Bedlam and no lady would ever admit that such
a thing had happened. You are trying to make me cry off

and it won't do. I do not give up what I consider to be mine."

Ashbourne looked at his daughter. "He has a point. It does sound like nonsense, Emily. Tell us the truth, Mr. Langford. What really happened?"

Philip had no trouble understanding Miss Ashbourne's desperation to be rid of her unwelcome suitor. And to feel that being ruined by having been in Bedlam to be a superior fate than marriage to this man.

Truth be told, he felt a strong desire to plant his fist in Canfield's face. To draw his cork and then to do the same to Miss Ashbourne's father.

Instead he glanced at his fingernails then up at Mr. Ashbourne. With something of a sneer he said, "Oh, it is true, I assure you. Miss Ashbourne made such a nuisance of herself, attempting to storm the doors of White's and accosting a member of the House of Lords, that the gentlemen present felt they had no choice but to have her carted off to Bedlam. I found her there myself."

Canfield gaped at Philip. His mouth opened and shut several times. He looked as though he could not decide whether to believe him or not. Finally he seemed to decide it didn't matter. He rose to his feet and glared at both father and daughter.

"Very well, Miss Ashbourne, you have won. If you can call it a victory. I shall send a notice to the papers that our betrothal is at an end. People will presume what they wish. Mr. Ashbourne, I wish you joy of your daughter. Good day to both of you!"

There was silence in the room until he was gone. Indeed until all four could hear the front door close behind him. Then they each spoke, according to their own view of the matter.

"Well, I think you are well shut of him, Miss Ashbourne."

"Thank you, Mr. Langford!"

"Emily, this time you have gone too far! And you,

Agatha! How could you let it happen? And you, Mr. Langford, how dare you have the impertinence to congratulate my daughter on whistling down the wind the most eligible suitor who has ever offered for her?"

"How, sir, could you allow your daughter to become betrothed to a man like that?" Philip countered, his anger rising.

Mr. Ashbourne regarded him with patent malevolence. "What right has a mere barrister to question any decisions I make? Unless, sir, you learn to respect your betters, you will have a very short career indeed!"

That did it. Any reserve of calm or rational thought deserted Philip. He took a step toward Mr. Ashbourne and was pleased to see the man back away.

"I? Respect my betters? My birth, I would hazard, is better than your own! Were I to tell you my brother's title, I wager you would recognize it at once."

But Philip's words did not have the effect he intended. Instead of intimidating Mr. Ashbourne, the man had first stared wide-eyed, stunned, then begun to smile enthusiastically. By the time he finished speaking, Philip had a strong sense that somehow he had just dug himself a very deep hole and was going to have a great deal of trouble climbing out.

He was right.

"Your brother's a lord, is he? Well, well, that puts an entirely different complexion on things. How is your dear brother?"

"Fine," Philip answered cautiously.

Now it was he who was backing up as Ashbourne advanced. The man had something in mind and Philip did not think he was going to like it.

He was right again.

"You seem to have taken quite an interest in my daughter."

"She asked for some legal advice and I was happy to be of service."

"Of course. And you have called often to see her here?"

Some instinct for self-preservation made Philip reply, "Occasionally."

"I see." Abruptly the mild geniality vanished and Ashbourne turned on the offensive. He wagged a finger in front of Philip's nose and demanded sternly, "What, sir, are your intentions toward my daughter?"

Philip gaped at the man. He couldn't think of anything except that perhaps Mr. Ashbourne, perhaps the entire family, belonged in Bedlam!

"Papa!"

"Jonathan! Really, Mr. Langford has been all that is kind and helpful to Emily. And to me. It is not right, it is not right at all, for you to repay him this way," Miss Jarrod said with some asperity.

To Philip's surprise, it worked. Miss Jarrod's words seemed to reach Ashbourne and he once again abruptly changed face. He dropped his hand from in front of Philip's face and shrugged.

"Oh, very well. But it seemed worth trying. What else am I to do about Emily? It's all very well for you, young man, to say she is well shut of Canfield, but what are we to do now? She has ruined herself twice over and I won't even have the funds Canfield promised to give me as consolation."

He paused and turned toward his daughter. "I wash my hands of you! Of you and Agatha! You wanted to ruin yourself? Well you have succeeded! Agatha, you can go and find another relative to live with. I'll have you upon my hands no longer. Emily, you'll pack your bags and be ready to leave here within the hour. I know a family desperate for a governess and they'll take you despite your reputation."

The look on Miss Ashbourne's face was sufficient to tell Philip that she knew the family her father meant. And that the prospect of going there was appalling to her. He didn't know what he was going to do until suddenly he found himself stepping between Mr. Ashbourne and his daughter.

Miss Ashbourne reached out a hand to stop Philip and he turned and smiled reassuringly to her. He caught the hand she was reaching out and used it to draw her to his side. And then he put his arm around her waist.

To Mr. Ashbourne he said, "I have an alternative suggestion, sir. Let your daughter become betrothed to me."

Mr. Ashbourne looked distinctly taken aback. Then he leaned forward, peering into Philip's face. Even Miss Ashbourne was gaping up at him.

"Did you say you rescued Emily from Bedlam or that you were in there with her?" Ashbourne demanded when he finally found his voice.

Philip flushed. It did not help that Miss Jarrod sighed, smiled warmly at him, and clasped her hands together as she said, "I knew they would suit, I just knew it and I prayed every day that they would realize it themselves. And now they have."

Only Miss Ashbourne did not speak and Philip had the oddest notion that it was because she could not. But her father spoke more than enough for the both of them.

"Well, well, well," he said, rubbing his hands together. "This puts another face on matters entirely! What a sly puss you are, Emily, not to give me a hint of what you were about! The brother of a lord. Well, well, perhaps it's not such a bad thing you routed Canfield, after all. Marriage settlements. We ought to talk about marriage settlements, Langford."

Now Miss Ashbourne found her voice. "No, Papa! Enough of this nonsense!"

She turned to Philip. "I had no notion, Mr. Langford, that you aspired to be a writer as well as a barrister. Your imagination is beyond anything I have ever read. It surpasses even Mr. Jonathan Swift's prodigious talent. What on earth makes you believe that I would agree to such a betrothal? I should rather be a governess than have you sacrifice yourself to a loveless match between us."

Now Philip gaped at her. Didn't she understand he was trying to help her? He opened his mouth to answer, but Miss Ashbourne whirled on her father before he had a chance to speak.

"And you, Papa! How can you countenance such a match? If you think Mr. Langford can make me respectable again, you much mistake the matter!"

At that, her father began to look alarmed. He cleared his throat. He colored up. He turned a fierce gaze on Philip and demanded to know if this was true.

"Could you make Emily respectable again?"

"I think so," Philip said. "Surely it cannot hurt to let me try."

For a long moment, Ashbourne was silent. Then he nodded to himself and said to Philip, "Very well. If you succeed, you may marry my daughter. But only if you succeed."

"Papa!"

"An excellent notion. Why, Emily, I have never known your father to be so sensible," Miss Jarrod said with patent approval, if not with any degree of tact.

"Aunt Agatha, I will not marry Mr. Langford!"

The conversation swirled on as if they had not heard her.

"Thank you, sir."

"Don't thank me yet. No notice is to be sent to the papers until Emily is respectable again. And I shall stay in London to see that no one tries to pull the wool over my eyes this time!"

That set off another round of protests. "Papa, no! We don't need you here."

"There really isn't a great deal of room, Jonathan."

In the midst of the confusion, Philip gently drew Miss Ashbourne aside. In a low voice, meant only for her ears, he said, "I know you cannot like this and it is not precisely what I would choose, either. But think! If your father believes you to be all but betrothed to me, he won't throw your aunt out in the street or make you become a governess! Later you can cry off. But for now, let me help you."

She stared up at him with her large blue eyes, searching his face. She wanted to accept his help, he could see it in her eyes. But she also felt she should refuse. For his sake. That, too, was clear in her eyes. There was a great deal he would have said to her, if he could, but with her aunt and father in the room, Philip could only squeeze Miss Ashbourne's hand in reassurance.

And then, slowly she nodded.

Emily felt as though she could scarcely breathe. Until the moment when Mr. Langford had offered to become betrothed to her, she could not have guessed how much she would want to agree. Or how much it would hurt to know he was only offering to do so in order to protect her, that he meant it as a temporary solution.

It was a most disconcerting discovery. Emily had not depended on anyone else for many years. And yet, in the short time she had been in London, she had come to depend on Mr. Langford far more than comfort would allow, far more than she could believe was wise.

And yet, what else was she to do? If she did not go along with this scheme, Papa would most certainly force her to become a governess and, worse, throw Aunt Agatha out on her own.

Emily could not envision either possibility with anything other than foreboding. So now, knowing it was foolish, knowing she ought not to trust this man who was all but a stranger to her, she nodded. And from the smile that suddenly lit up his face, Emily took even greater alarm than before.

For once, perhaps, she was wise.

Chapter 12

Philip cursed himself all the way home. What the devil had he been thinking? Not only had he offered for a girl who was nothing but trouble, and not in the least likely to advance his career, but he had done so twice over!

He had not even had the sense to draw back when she protested and he had the opportunity to do so. It would have been such an easy thing to imply that Miss Ashbourne was right and that he could not possibly make her respectable again. And it might very well have been the truth! But he had not done so.

Granted, he had made it clear to Miss Ashbourne that this was a spurious betrothal, meant only to protect her until she resolved matters in some other way, nevertheless it was most unlike him to do such a thing. When had he developed this chivalrous steak in his nature? It was most disconcerting and uncomfortably like what he could remember of his father. And what his brothers would say, when they learned of this latest start, was more than Philip cared to think about.

His brothers! George! Good heavens, what was he going to do when Emily and George met, for the first time, in his company? Despite the warmth of the day, Philip began to feel quite cold.

He would just, he told himself firmly, have to make certain that George and Miss Ashbourne did not meet. At least not for a very long time.

As for James and Harry, well, they could be trusted to understand, he thought, were it not for that damnable pact the three had made not to marry. He could tell them it was a false betrothal, meant only to pacify Miss Ashbourne's father. The trouble was, Philip found himself oddly reluctant to do so. He was, he realized, actually considering not drawing back from this betrothal. And that thought frightened Philip more than anything else could have done.

So intent was he on these thoughts that he did not at first notice the confusion when he reached Gray's Inn. Nor would he have at all had not one of the other barristers hailed him and asked, "Have you heard the latest news? There was a fierce battle in the Peninsula! The casualty lists are to be posted at any time now."

Instantly his own concerns were forgotten in his fear for Harry. "Where?" he demanded.

His friend named a town that meant nothing to Philip. Nor did he know which regiments had been involved.

"But we've won the battle, that much I know!" he overheard someone say exultantly.

Philip hoped it was true. But the price would be too high if victory came at the cost of his brother's life. Not for the first time, he damned his brother for bullying George into buying him a pair of colors.

Still, with victory in the air, his was not a popular sentiment and so Philip kept it to himself. He retreated to his office, after extracting a promise from his friend to come and fetch him the moment there was news.

But five minutes, listening to the uproar outside his door, was sufficient to prove to Philip that this would not do. Restless, he rose to his feet and left Gray's Inn. If he could do nothing to speed the posting of the lists, at least, perhaps, he could do something about Miss Ashbourne's fortunes. It was time he truly was of service to her and perhaps his efforts on her behalf would hold at bay, at least for a little while, his fears for Harry.

Besides, for the first time since he had spoken, he understood part of the impulse that had led him to do so, and it had to do with Harry and Harry's questions about Richard Canfield. As Miss Ashbourne's fiancé he could visit her home and perhaps inspect the mill Canfield owned. He could speak with her friends who worked there and perhaps discover something that would help Harry.

But first he had to make Miss Ashbourne respectable.

It went against the grain with him, but Philip's manners were every bit as polished as James's when he chose. And today he chose to be charming and gallant with every dowager, every matron he knew who might possibly be willing to extend an invitation to Miss Ashbourne.

It would never have occurred to Philip to wonder at his success. After all, from birth he was accustomed to being liked. And being able to persuade others to do as he wished. Still, even he ought not to have expected all of the ladies he approached to agree to his request.

What he did not know was that each and every one of those ladies found herself intrigued by his concern for Miss Ashbourne. Indeed each one felt a certain satisfaction at knowing that some young lady, any young lady, had finally caught the attention of a young man who had long since been the despair of every matchmaking mama in London.

Had they been gentlemen, these ladies would have been making wagers at White's as to the likelihood that Mr. Philip Langford was likely to be leg-shackled at last. Since they were not, they merely indulged in a little gossip with their bosom bows, once he was gone.

And that was how, in the space of a few hours, all of London learned that the Honorable Philip Langford had fallen into the clutches of a young lady no one in London had seen. At least not in six years. And those acquaintances who had brushed aside Miss Jarrod's requests for help in launching her niece, suddenly were sending around invitations, apologizing that they had not been sent out sooner.

Miss Ashbourne and Miss Jarrod found themselves surrounded by a bewildering number of choices and a sinking sensation that it all had to do with a certain gentleman who had, perhaps, not been as discreet as he ought.

And they were right.

"What a fortunate thing it is that you ordered these ball gowns," Miss Jarrod said as she eyed her niece later that evening. "Rose is a most becoming color for you."

"Is it?" Emily asked doubtfully as she stared into the mirror. "I feel like a hothouse flower. Something to be admired but scarcely touched for fear I shall fall apart if anyone does so."

"Nonsense!" Mr. Ashbourne said stoutly. "You look charming, absolutely charming. Just as you ought. If you had ever consented to dress like this at home, perhaps you would have been married years ago and I should have a grandchild to dandle on my knees."

More alarmed than ever, Emily began to back away, toward the stairs, her eyes wide. "Perhaps we shouldn't go tonight. Perhaps I ought to stay here and go to bed early. I know we shan't have any fun and you, dear Aunt Agatha, surely you have the headache?"

But these tactics, however well they might have worked at home, did not fare so well here in London. Not now, when her father had the bit between his teeth.

"You'll go tonight," he said sternly, "and no more nonsense about it! Your mama would have said it was just the thing and what's more, she would have been right."

The mention of her mother acted upon Emily as her father knew it would. She went very still, very pale. He pressed his advantage.

"You look very like her, you know. Particularly tonight. She loved to dance. Thought me a clumsy fool because I couldn't. But she married me anyway, and very happy we were, until she died. Trying to say you oughtn't to look for perfection. Now come along. Your Mr. Langford will be here any minute and you'd best be ready. You, too, Agatha. Not in the first blush of youth anymore, but you'll do credit to me and to Emily tonight, too."

Miss Jarrod blushed and shook her head, but it was easy to see that she was pleased. As if to prove Ashbourne right, the knocker sounded a moment later and Mr. Langford was admitted to the house.

He paused at the sight of the Ashbourne party and Emily was woman enough to be pleased at the way his jaw dropped at the sight of her. It was shock, but an admiring shock, for his mouth snapped shut into a smile and his eyes began to dance as he looked at her.

And then he bowed. Deeply, elegantly, as if she were a royal princess and not some troublesome creature he kept having to rescue.

"Well, Langford," Ashbourne demanded impatiently, "will she do?"

"She will," Mr. Langford answered, keeping his eyes on Emily, "take the *ton* by storm. Yes, sir, she will most definitely do."

"Very nicely said," Aunt Agatha said with a sharp nod of approval. "Now come along, we mustn't be late."

Now Mr. Langford turned to look at the older woman. There was mischief in his voice as he said, "Ah, but don't you know that it is fashionable to be late? To make an entrance? As we will?"

Aunt Agatha merely snorted but Emily knew her well enough to know when she was pleased. And she was very pleased with Mr. Langford.

Well, Emily could understand that. She was rather pleased with the man, herself. And also a little afraid. He turned to her and held out a hand.

"Your aunt is right," he said softly, "we should be going."

Softly! He spoke to her softly, as if she were a horse that needed gentling! Emily wanted to slap him for his presumption, even as she found herself reaching out and placing her hand in his. Perhaps being gentled wasn't such a terrible notion, after all.

He smiled, but it was not a smile of triumph; rather it was a smile meant to reassure. He tucked her hand into the crook of his elbow and then turned to offer his other arm to Aunt Agatha, who took it with a self-conscious smile of her own.

"Are you coming with us, sir?" Mr. Langford asked Emily's father.

Mr. Ashbourne lifted an eyebrow. " 'Course I'm coming!" he snapped. "Think I'd be dressed like this if I wasn't? Someone has to keep an eye on the lot of you! Agatha's a good woman, I don't say that she's not. But my girl has been able to get around her since the very first. And you, sir, have yet to prove to my satisfaction, that I've not just set the cat among the pigeons by encouraging you to make free with this house and escorting my daughter."

Emily held her breath, waiting for Mr. Langford to take offense. But he did not. Instead he answered with cool disdain, "Quite right. In your position I should be just as cautious. Shall we go?"

But the way he squeezed her hand reassuringly, with his elbow, belied the chill of his words. And when he looked down at her, it was with such warmth in his eyes that Emily had to lower hers in confusion.

He showed both ladies every courtesy as he handed first Aunt Agatha and then Emily into his carriage. Nor was it the hollow gesture of a practiced dandy but rather a genuine concern for their welfare that prompted this.

Or so it seemed to Emily. At which point she scolded herself for a fool and sternly determined to be more on her guard. What, after all, did she know of practiced dandies? Nothing, she had to allow, save that she did not think they often had such warmth in their eyes, such concern in their voices as they talked with the women they were charming. The gestures might have been the same, but it would all have been done in a way that left no doubt it was a game to them. And it did not seem to be a game to Mr. Langford at all.

Nor did his attentiveness flag once they reached Lady Merriweather's town house. Emily had the oddest sensation of being protected and shielded as he helped her to navigate between the people gathered there and led their party up to Lady Merriweather and her daughter.

"May I present Miss Jarrod, Miss Ashbourne, and Mr. Ashbourne?" he said to the hostess.

Lady Merriweather was pleased to be gracious once she saw that Emily was much older and therefore no threat to her own daughter, in whose honor this ball was being held.

Nor did he abandon her after this. He led the Ashbourne party to a quiet side of the room where Aunt Agatha could sit. And he was so obliging as to point Emily's father in the direction of the card rooms. Then he smiled at her and held out a hand.

"Shall we dance?"

Emily allowed him to lead her to where the lines were being formed for the next country dance. She caught a sideways glance that told her Mr. Langford was wondering if she would feel out of place.

She might have reassured him, but preferred to see his look of surprise, if surprise it was, when he discovered that in this, at least, she was as accomplished as any London-raised girl. Perhaps one day they would know one another well enough that she could confide how, as a child, dancing had been her one joy and her dancing instructor the one person who had not laughed at her odd notions or tried to squelch the streak of rebelliousness that had always been part of her nature.

Chapter 13

Philip watched as Miss Ashbourne moved gracefully through the figures of the dance. For the first time since he had met her, she looked as if she had really come alive and he wondered at the change in her. But it was a change of which he thoroughly approved.

And because there was no chance for them to speak, he let his eyes also watch for the reactions to her presence here. Fortunately his brother George did not seem to be in attendance. Nor anyone else who might recognize Miss Ashbourne as the lady clapped up into Bedlam.

Then he gave himself up to the pleasure of dancing with a lovely young woman. One who did not expect him to feed her empty compliments at every opportunity, but who was content simply to be in his company as they danced. It came to Philip that when Miss Ashbourne was not pressing her cause, she was a remarkably restful woman in whose company to find oneself.

And when it was over, he led her back to her aunt, then excused himself to see which acquaintances he could persuade to dance with her next. It was not such a difficult task as he anticipated.

"Dance with a girl? One you came with? Delighted, Langford, simply delighted!"

And if there was too much mischief in the smile, how could Philip cavil at it? But he did draw the line at answering impertinent questions.

"What is the girl to you, Langford? Never known you to take an interest in the petticoat line before."

"Who is she and how do you come to know her? Haven't seen her about before, have I?"

"Trying to put the tabbies off the scent, are you? Useless thing to try to do, you know. They'll be making wagers at White's by tomorrow morning."

And so it went. But they danced with Miss Ashbourne. And spoke kindly of her afterward. So much so that at times Philip had to keep his tongue clenched between his teeth. He watched, moreover, with mixed emotions, as some of his friends asked Miss Ashbourne for a second dance, all of their own accord.

As for him, Philip knew he dared not provoke more gossip than could be helped by trying to dance with her more than twice himself. Or by dancing only with Miss Ashbourne. So he chose, almost at random, some young ladies to dance with, making certain, however, that it was he who partnered her for the supper dance.

"Are you enjoying yourself, Miss Ashbourne?" Philip asked with, a smile as he led her to the room where the tables had been set up.

She smiled back up at him unaware, he would have sworn, of how much pleasure her glowing face betrayed. "Oh, yes, Mr. Langford!"

"I vow my niece has not sat out a single dance," Miss Jarrod, who had come in to supper with them, added, with no small note of pride in her voice.

Philip went to fetch them both plates and was surprised, when he returned to the table to discover that another gentleman had joined them. He was even more surprised to realize that it was Sir Thomas Levenger.

"Sit, m'boy. I'm renewing my acquaintance with an old friend," Sir Thomas said, smiling at Miss Jarrod who, to Philip's surprise, blushed.

He glanced at Miss Ashbourne, who appeared to be

equally fascinated. Sir Thomas? With a woman? No doubt Miss Ashbourne was thinking, Aunt Agatha? With a man?

It was an interesting development and one that Philip could only applaud. This was a sentiment patently shared by Miss Ashbourne, who looked at him with merriment in her eyes as Sir Thomas addressed Miss Jarrod.

"Perhaps, Miss Jarrod, you would favor me with another dance after supper?"

"Another dance?" Philip echoed the words aloud.

Sir Thomas quirked an eyebrow at him. "Yes, another dance. Do you find it so hard to imagine that I know how to do so?"

"No, not at all," Philip hastily replied.

Sir Thomas turned back to smile at Miss Jarrod, who blushed again. "I should like that," she said with becoming reserve.

"Careful, Aunt Agatha," Miss Ashbourne said teasingly. "If you dance more than twice with Sir Thomas, you will have tongues wagging!"

Another woman might have taken alarm and drawn back. Miss Jarrod, to Philip's amusement, merely straightened, looked at her niece, and said loftily, "Let them wag. I am past the age of having to worry about such things. Besides, I shan't listen to any gossip and neither will you."

"That's the spirit!" Sir Thomas said approvingly.

He beamed at Miss Jarrod and she at him. The two left the table before Miss Ashbourne and Philip were done.

The moment they were gone, Miss Ashbourne looked around to see that no one was listening, then said, "All right, I am here. And I have danced until my feet hurt. But I have yet to see one member of the House of Lords who could be useful to me. The few here are unrelenting enemies of the sort of change I am urging."

Philip grinned at the fierceness in her expression. "Peace, child," he said, fanning the flames with his teasing. "It is a beginning. You need to go out and about and then, when you are in company, and you see the gentlemen you need to speak with, they are less likely to shy away from you. For they will think you as harmless as their wives and sisters and mothers."

Her eyes narrowed, as though she wondered if he were merely fobbing her off with some tale. But then she nodded. "Perhaps you are right. The best generals say that to win a battle, it is a great advantage if one can catch the enemy off guard."

Philip burst out laughing; he could not help himself. "What do you know of generals and battles and armies?" he asked.

"As much as you do, I should wager!" Miss Ashbourne snapped.

She reeled off the names of a number of texts on the subject of war. Philip sobered quickly as he realized she meant she had read them all.

His own face darkened as he thought of Harry and he said, when she paused to take a breath, "So you have read books. Have you known anyone who came back from a war?"

She shook her head. He went on. "I have, Miss Ashbourne. My brother Harry is fighting in the Peninsula. Even now I am waiting to hear the casualty lists of yet another battle to know if this time he survived or was hurt or killed. So when you speak of war you ought to know that it is not a game, a series of words in a book, but a grim reality. In war there is a real cost to every battle, to every decision, whether right or wrong."

He had angered her, though he never meant to do so. Her voice was grim as she replied, low so that she would not be overheard, "So, too, there is a cost in what I do! You rescued me from Bedlam, but do you have any notion what the hours were like for me, while I was there? And I was fortunate! Lord Darton could have had me sent to jail. Have you ever visited a prison, Mr. Langford? I have. You may laugh at me, at my naiveté in thinking I can change the world. But do not pretend to me that what I do has no cost!"

Abruptly his own mood changed and his hand shot out to grasp her wrist. "What did happen to you in Bedlam?" he demanded.

Gently, firmly, implacably, she freed her wrist. And she managed to do so without drawing the eyes of those around them, no mean feat given his mood.

She placed her hands in her lap and met his eyes squarely as she said, "I shall never tell you. Or anyone else. And no, it is not what you most fear. But it was bad enough, all the same."

He wanted to demand she tell him more, but there was a look in her eyes that somehow told him there was no way that he could make her do so.

Instead, he rose to his feet and bowed. "Miss Ashbourne," he asked, in a cold and distant voice, "shall I escort you back to the ballroom?"

She looked away and then back at him. She opened her mouth to speak, then closed it again. Finally she rose to her feet and placed her hand in his.

"Yes."

Miss Jarrod was dancing with Sir Thomas and Philip could not abandon Miss Ashbourne, however many tabbies there were willing to look after her.

"Shall we take a walk around the room and perhaps peek into the card rooms?" he asked, instead. "Perhaps we shall catch a glimpse of your father."

She nodded eagerly. Too eagerly, Philip thought in confusion. He was right to be wary. The second room they looked in, she gave a tiny exclamation by his side. But why? Her father wasn't in the room. Philip wasn't left in doubt for very long. Miss Ashbourne told him.

"There is Lord Beaumont. He is a potential ally. I am told he is sympathetic to causes such as ours."

Ours? When had her cause become "ours" in her mind?

But Philip had no time to ponder the matter. Instead he had to stop her, for she was marching toward the table where Lord Beaumont sat, playing piquet.

There was no time for discretion, no time to be polite. Philip grabbed Miss Ashbourne's arm and swung her back around so that she was facing the doorway again.

"Not now! Not here!" he hissed at her as he continued to push her out of the room.

"But you said I should speak to men such as Lord Beaumont at social events," she protested indignantly. "Isn't that why you said I should come?"

Philip wished he could mop his brow, but that would have drawn far too much attention to them. "Not here, not now," he repeated, a hint of desperation in his voice. "While you are dancing or perhaps over a glass of wine in the supper room. Times like that is what I meant. I never meant that you should interrupt a game of cards and draw everyone's attention to yourself."

"But how can I talk to Lord Beaumont on the dance floor or in the supper room if he never comes in there?" she asked reasonably. "What am I supposed to do if he spends the entire evening playing cards?"

"Wait for another opportunity, another night, another ball," Philip replied in exasperation.

"And if I choose not to do so?" she demanded.

"Then I shall wash my hands of you," Philip retorted, meaning every word.

"But you promised to help me!"

"Only so long as you show at least some shred of discretion," he warned her.

She wanted to challenge him, he could read it in her eyes, in the very way she stood, chin tilted up toward him. But in the end she did not.

"I suppose you are right," she said with a tiny sigh. "You had best take me back to my aunt. The dance is over and she will no doubt be sitting among the chaperones again by now."

Philip was happy to take her back to Miss Jarrod. If he could have found her. But another gentleman had already asked her to dance and he found himself in a quandary, for he could not simply abandon Miss Ashbourne and yet the longer he stayed by her side, the more gossip there would be.

Fortunately, a gentleman came to ask her to dance and Philip was able to retreat to find a partner for himself. He made himself stay away from Miss Ashbourne for the rest of the evening, save when the figures of the dance brought them together.

She had no shortage of partners, he noted grimly. Nor did her aunt, which made him look at the woman a little closer and realize that she was not quite as old as he had first assumed. She must have been much younger than her sister, Miss Ashbourne's mother.

Well, it was none of Philip's affair. All he had to do was make certain Miss Ashbourne did not land herself in the suds. And it would no doubt take all his energy just to manage that.

Indeed, Philip felt a distinct sense of impending disaster when he realized that she was dancing with Lord Beaumont and that whenever she came close enough, spoke earnestly to the man. Lord Beaumont looked distinctly alarmed and Philip felt an impulse to intervene. But it was impossible. He could not. Philip and his partner were in another group and it would have created far too great a sensation were he to leave his position and join theirs.

To be sure, Lord Beaumont did not seem terribly disturbed, when at last the dance ended, but Philip could not help noting how quickly the man returned Miss Ashbourne to her aunt and made good his escape, not only from her, but from the ball as well.

With a sigh, Philip decided that perhaps it was time to

take the Ashbournes home. With that thought in mind, he went in search of her father.

He found him in the card room. Winning. Philip knew what that meant. Ashbourne would be all but impossible to pry loose from the table. Still, he had to try.

To his surprise, the man came at once. He was even more surprised when Ashbourne explained why. "Doesn't do to stay at the tables too long when you're winning, m'boy. Luck always turns. Best to leave before it does."

Since this seemed to Philip a most sensible philosophy, he could think of nothing to say. The ladies were less pleased to be leaving, but they made no actual protest.

Indeed, Miss Ashbourne confided that she felt a little tired, as he handed her into the carriage waiting outside.

"I am not accustomed to such late hours," she said, leaning back against the squabs.

Her father laughed self-consciously. "Now, puss," he said, "you mustn't be giving Mr. Langford the notion that you are hopelessly countrified!"

"On the contrary, she gives me the impression of having a great deal of sense," Philip said, instantly coming to her defense.

And then, alarmed at discovering yet again such a chivalrous impulse in himself, he fell silent. As did the others. What the devil was the matter with him?

Philip was distinctly relieved to let the Ashbourne party down at their hired house, though he allowed not a trace of this to show in his voice. But the first thing he did when he arrived at his own was to pour himself a very large glass of brandy.

Philip had no notion what was happening to him, but he was quite certain he did not like it. When had he come to feel so much concern for Miss Ashbourne? He thought himself safe from the fairer sex. His brother George's wife had provided all the example he needed to be wary of such entanglements.

And yet, apparently it was not enough. Philip poured himself a second brandy, but even that was not enough to let him sleep. Some hours later, he found himself watching the dawn come up, no closer to an answer than before.

Chapter 14

Lord Beaumont did not quite know what to think of the young lady who had accosted him the night before. On the one hand, she took an unseemly interest in matters that ladies should know nothing about, and she had talked to him about it at a ball! On the other hand, she clearly knew first-hand of the things she told him.

Since he had not been present the day the madwoman accosted Lord Darton outside of White's, Lord Beaumont had no notion they were one and the same. As a result he congratulated himself that he was luckier than his colleague. At least he had a lady to deal with and one who was remarkably pretty.

It was also true that Lord Beaumont had made something of a career out of championing the poor. It made him different from his fellow members of the House of Lords. And he even managed to believe, in a passing sort of way, in the causes he took up.

But until now, the people affected had never touched his own reality. If he won, he celebrated. If he lost, he shrugged and went on to the next cause. Beaumont had a shrewd notion, however, that if he took up Miss Ashbourne's cause, she would not allow him to relinquish it easily.

If he accepted her challenge, she would expect him to follow through until he succeeded in changing the law. And no one, he thought gloomily, could suppose that would be easy! Or quick. No, it would be far wiser to tell her that he was too busy with the causes he already championed to take up hers. That would be the sensible thing to do.

And yet, her urgency, her concern touched that very core of Lord Beaumont which had led him to adopt the pose of crusader in the first place. The part of him that cared more than his peers, the part of him that was human enough to be able to imagine what it would be like to be someone without the advantages he and his peers had been born to possess.

By the end of the morning, Lord Beaumont knew, with a sinking feeling, that he was well and truly caught in Miss Ashbourne's snare. He only hoped someone would join him there and he would not turn out to be pursuing a hopeless cause alone. Who, he wondered, could he enlist to help him?

On the other side of town, Emily was making a botch of her needlework.

"What is the trouble, dear?" Aunt Agatha asked kindly.

Emily glanced over at her father, who seemed engrossed in going over the bills. Still, one could not presume he was not listening. She bit her lower lip and hesitated. Her aunt seemed to understand perfectly and she nodded decisively.

"Come, Emily, I need to purchase more silk thread to finish these handkerchiefs. I should like your help in matching them in the shop."

Immediately Emily rose to her feet. "Of course," she said, heading for the door. "It will only take me a moment to fetch my bonnet and spencer."

"It will take a trifle longer than that for me to get ready," Aunt Agatha replied tartly, but there was no real annoyance in her voice.

Ten minutes later, they were walking down the street in the direction of the nearest shops. "Do you really need silks?" Emily asked her aunt.

Agatha smiled and shook her head, her eyes twinkling with mischief. "No, but we had better buy some, all the same. One never knows what your father may or may not notice. And as we walk, you must tell me what is troubling you."

Emily hesitated for a long moment. Not entirely certain, herself, what was wrong. At last she said, staring down at her feet, unable to meet her aunt's eyes. "I suppose it is Mr. Langford."

She waited but Aunt Agatha did not speak and, after a moment, Emily went on. "I know it is foolish to repine too much upon his proposal. I know he does not mean to marry me, that it was a chivalrous gesture to protect me. For a little while. Until I can find some other solution to my dilemma. A gesture he no doubt regretted the moment it was made."

"But?"

Emily turned to her aunt and looked at her with haunted eyes. "But a part of me wishes he did mean it, Aunt Agatha. And I am very much afraid he will read it in my face. And it is not right. I ought not to wish for more than he has been so generous to give!"

Aunt Agatha smiled, but there was an edge of exasperation to her voice as she said, "Whatever gave you the notion that the heart listens to reason? Or to what is right or wrong? Do you think mine listened when I loved a man my family considered totally ineligible? Or that when I obeyed my parents and refused to run away with him, it would listen when I tried to tell it to fix an interest on someone else? Someone of whom they could approve? No," she said, shaking her head vehemently, "the heart loves as it will. And I am not so certain it is wrong to do so. Perhaps Mr. Langford will feel obliged, in the end, to carry through with his proposal and marry you after all."

Now there was exasperation in Emily's voice as she replied, "That is what I fear, Aunt Agatha! Mr. Langford has been so kind as to offer me his protection. For the moment. It would be a wicked turn I would serve him if I actually held him to his proposal. But I fear I shall be sorely tempted to do so."

Agatha awkwardly patted her niece's shoulder. "You have too much strength of character to do such a thing. But why are you so certain he does not feel something of the same? I should have said he did."

Emily only shook her head.

Aunt Agatha sighed. "Well, if you do not marry Mr. Langford, what will you do?"

"That," she confessed, "is what troubles me the most. I do not know. I suppose I ought to be looking about me for another possible husband. But I cannot like the useless fribbles who have danced with me. Or the ones who are pompous beyond belief. Or the older gentlemen who remind me far too much of Papa. There has not been one gentleman I could even contemplate as a husband!"

"Except Mr. Langford."

"Except Mr. Langford," Emily miserably agreed.

They turned into the shop that sold the embroidery silks and spent some time picking out just the right colors. It was a pleasurable occupation and one that gave Emily the time her aunt judged she required to sort out her own thoughts.

On the way home she waited for Emily to raise the subject once again. Which she did. "Is it always like this?" she asked.

"What do you mean?" Agatha asked cautiously.

Emily hesitated. "I know I ought to be thinking of the mill workers and the need to make things better for them. It was, after all, my purpose in coming to London. And I am not even certain Mr. Langford truly supports me in this. But there are long moments when I forget entirely."

Her aunt could be seen visibly struggling to keep from laughing. A circumstance that did not improve Emily's temper in the least.

"My dear child, I had forgotten what it was to be so young!" Agatha gasped.

Emily gritted her teeth. "I am three and twenty," she reminded her aunt.

"Yes, and entirely inexperienced in love," Agatha declared decisively. "My dear Emily, what you are feeling is perfectly natural when you love someone!"

"But I don't want to be in love," Emily countered.

This, of course, was fuel for further amusement on Aunt Agatha's part. "I told you before, one has no control, or at least very little, over such things. But very well, I shall be serious. Tell me, Emily, if Mr. Langford did wish to marry you, would you wish to marry him?"

Emily turned wide, bewildered eyes on her aunt. "I don't know," she said, the words holding a thin wail of pain running through her voice. "At times I think Mr. Langford wonderful! Everything one could wish for in a husband. At others I wish nothing more than to strangle the man!"

Agatha nodded. "Very sensible, and natural, I should think," she said approvingly.

Despite herself, Emily gave a little gurgle of laughter. "Aunt Agatha, you are outrageous!" she said, taking her aunt's arm.

"Why?" Agatha demanded. "Because I speak my mind? Well, I refuse to do anything else! Which is another reason, I suppose," she said with a tiny sigh, "that I have never married. I have known only one man in my life who could accept a woman as outspoken as I am."

"The same mysterious man you mentioned before?" Emily asked dryly. When her aunt nodded, Emily persisted, "Sir Thomas Levenger, I suppose? No, you needn't frown at me like that—I overheard Papa talking, more than once, when you first came. They thought I wouldn't understand. But why? He seems a most eligible suitor."

"Not then he wasn't. It is only now that he is a judge that he is everywhere received. His background is not quite the thing, though no one looking at him could ever guess! And so I have always said."

There was a sadness, a wistfulness, in Aunt Agatha's voice that tugged at Emily's heart and she instinctively slipped her arm around her aunt's shoulders. "But there must have come a time when you could have married him. Whether your family approved or not." A thought struck her and she said with some dismay, "It was not because of me, was it? Because Mama had died and you felt you must take care of me?"

Agatha looked away. She blinked rapidly and shook her head. "Oh, no, you have not earned the right to question me in such a way. Nor shall you divert me so easily. We were talking about you. And Mr. Langford. I do understand your confusion, my dear. I even think you are wise to be wary. And yet there is something about Mr. Langford that makes one wish to trust him. Makes one believe that all would work out well if one did so."

Emily looked down. In a low voice she said, "I do find myself wishing to trust him. But what if I am wrong? As I was with Mr. Canfield?"

Aunt Agatha snorted. "There is nothing in common between the two! Well, save that they are both men and all men share certain weaknesses. But that is neither here nor there. What you mean is that you fear Mr. Langford may be lying to you and intending to deceive you, just as Mr. Canfield did. But the circumstances are very different, I should say. Mr. Canfield never rescued you, as Mr. Langford has done, more than once. Mr. Canfield set out to trap you so that you would have no choice in the matter of marrying him, but I cannot imagine Mr. Langford doing such a thing."

Emily said nothing for several moments. Finally, her voice still troubled, she looked at her aunt and asked, "If Sir Thomas were to ask you to marry him, would you?"

Agatha immediately stiffened and looked straight ahead, her pace suddenly much quicker. "You do not know what you are saying!" she said, her voice unsteady. "I hurt

Thomas greatly, years ago. He is not likely to ask me such a thing now, I assure you."

"But if he did?" Emily persisted.

Agatha drew in an audible breath. The hands clutching her parcel of embroidery silks shook. And when she did answer, her voice was pitched so low that Emily had to strain to hear her reply.

"If Sir Thomas were ever to be willing to overlook the past and ask me to marry him, I should agree at once. Yes, and," Agatha added, turning to Emily, her eyes flashing with an unaccustomed defiance, "I shouldn't care a jot what your father or anyone else thought. For once in my life, I would follow my heart!"

And then, as though appalled by what she had just said, but unwilling to take back her words, Agatha pressed her lips tightly together and tilted her chin defiantly upward.

Oblivious to and undaunted by any interested eyes, Emily gave her aunt a quick hug. With a fierceness that surprised both of them she said, "I hope Sir Thomas does propose, Aunt Agatha!"

But this was too much for her aunt, who shook her head and said, "Oh, no. It has been too long and he cannot still feel the same way about me that I feel about him."

"He was kind to you at Lady Merriweather's ball."

"It was the kindness of an old friend," Agatha said with a tremulous sigh. "That is all it was, all it could be. I will not, I must not, refine too greatly upon it! But you must not make the same mistake as I did, Emily. If your Mr. Langford should offer for you in earnest, you must accept him. The both of you will be miserable for the rest of your lives if you do not!"

Emily did not argue. It would only have distressed her aunt even more if she did. But it did not matter. Mr. Langford would not propose to her in earnest. And no more than her aunt did she intend to deceive herself with foolish, wishful thinking.

Emily had long since come to terms, she told herself, with the knowledge that she would never marry. It ought to be enough that she and Mr. Langford were friends and that he was willing to help her.

But there was a part of Emily that could not be sensible. A part of her that wondered where he was, this very moment, and what he was doing, and whether he was, perhaps, thinking of her.

Chapter 15

At that precise moment, Philip was glaring at his law books and cursing them for the sin of not being able to hold his attention. Unfortunately, a certain face kept intruding into his thoughts whenever he tried to concentrate on Sir Francis Bacon's treatise on the Statute of Uses. And a certain voice seemed to whisper in his ears.

And then, of course, there was Harry. What had seemed a victory they were now hearing was actually a defeat. Philip had read the latest lists and not seen Harry's name on any of them. That proved nothing, of course. He was somewhat reassured to have the letter in Harry's own hand in his desk, but how could he be certain it had been written after the battle was over? The devil take it, where was his brother now?

With a sigh Philip shoved his law books aside. Sir Thomas was hearing a case in court today and Philip had promised to be there to observe. Later they would talk it over and discuss the case endlessly, with Sir Thomas pressing him to find faults in how it had been presented.

Perhaps, he thought as he walked, he could speak of Miss Ashbourne to Sir Thomas, as he could not with his own brothers. Perhaps he would have some way of looking at the matter that had not yet occurred to Philip.

But first he had a case to observe. Sir Thomas was a judge now, but Philip found himself remembering the first time he had heard him speak. Even then he had instantly recognized Sir Thomas to be a master of oratory.

As Philip had slipped into the courtroom, he had taken note of the rapt faces around him, hanging on Sir Thomas's words as he thundered his outrage. And then softened his voice to speak of things almost too painful to bear.

Around him, Philip had heard a sniff and noted the discreet use of handkerchiefs. He had almost smiled, cynically, for Sir Thomas, when he invited him to come and observe, had described just how he would evoke such emotions. But Philip had not smiled.

Instead he had watched and listened and learned. It had been no surprise to anyone in the court when Sir Thomas won his case. And yet the man had not allowed a trace of triumph to cross his face, though that must have been what he felt. Instead he kept a sober mien and spoke, when he spoke at all, on his way out, of the seriousness of what had just occurred. He reminded those who asked, that a man's life had been at stake and that knowing it was now forfeit was not a matter for rejoicing so much as a matter for regret.

It was a very nice touch. Particularly since Philip well knew that though he did it deliberately, it also echoed what Sir Thomas truly felt. Which, of course, was no doubt one of the reasons it worked so well. One more thing Philip had taken note of that day.

But now Sir Thomas was a judge. A good one. And the Wentworth case far tamer than those he had dealt with as a barrister. But still Philip listened and learned.

And when court adjourned for the day, Sir Thomas smiled when he spied his favorite protégé standing outside, waiting for him.

"Well?" he asked when he was close enough. "What did you think?"

Philip grinned. "You were superb, as usual," he said promptly. "As you very well know."

Sir Thomas chuckled and clapped Philip on the back. "Wise fellow, you tell me just what I wish to hear. Which augurs well for your career as a barrister. Come, let us go and get something to eat. And you can tell me what you think of the points of law you heard argued today."

They repaired to a favorite tavern crowded with barristers and those involved in cases in the nearby courts. They managed to find a tiny corner to themselves. Something of Philip's preoccupation must have shown on his face for, between bites of food, Sir Thomas asked, "Worried about your brother Harry, are you? Saw the lists. Name wasn't on them."

"No, it wasn't," Philip agreed.

"But you still worry?"

"I always worry."

Sir Thomas wisely did not try to reassure Philip but merely nodded. "Let me know when you hear from him," was all he said. He paused then asked shrewdly, "So how is the reformer? Still as fiery as ever?"

Philip sighed. "You know," he said wryly, "I begin to think you sent Miss Ashbourne to me to be a constant thorn in my side."

Sir Thomas chuckled. "On the contrary, I sent her to you to liven up both your lives. Now tell me what is distressing you."

Reluctantly, Philip did so, feeling the burden ease slightly as he spoke. Sir Thomas was an excellent listener. Only when Philip was done did the elder barrister speak.

"You've a problem on your hands," he said quietly. "But one I shall relish watching you deal with."

"No advice?"

Sir Thomas shook his head. "No, on the whole, I think it will do you good to deal with such a thorny problem on your own. And all taken as one, I think you have matters well in hand."

Philip would have sputtered, but how did one object to having the person one admired most say that he had complete confidence in one? Still he tried.

There was a hint of malice in his voice as he said, "You

do realize that Miss Ashbourne believes that you, as a judge, could help her cause."

Sir Thomas merely regarded Philip sardonically. "If it comes to that," he said, "I should be perfectly willing to hear the case. If you prepared it correctly."

"There is no way to prepare such a thing correctly!" Philip snapped back in reply.

Sir Thomas merely shrugged. And then, before Philip could argue further, the elder man referred to the case he had been hearing in court today. He leaned forward, as always, and offered his usual opening question.

"Never mind all that, Langford, tell me about my case. What mistakes were made in court today?"

Philip sighed, knowing there was no way to deter Sir Thomas or to bring the conversation back around to Miss Ashbourne. So, with good grace, he smiled and leaned forward to answer.

Several nights later, Lord Darton glanced irritably at his wife. "Another ball? Can we not just stay at home? Or you go! I shall spend the evening at White's."

Athenia merely stared at her husband. "Stay at home?" she echoed incredulously. "When it is your brother's welfare at stake?"

"James?" Darton asked with a frown.

"No, Philip."

"Yes, well, Philip can take care of himself," Darton said irritably.

His wife smiled thinly and settled herself more firmly in the chair opposite him. "Not," she said, marshaling her arguments, "according to a number of ladies with whom I have spoken. It seems your brother Philip has taken up with the most unlikely of creatures. A complete provincial! They say he is absolutely smitten. She made a disgrace of herself six years ago when she was first brought out and now your brother Philip has made her the object of his attentions."

Darton did not take great stock in the suggestion that the young lady in question had been disgraced. In his experience, Athenia and other ladies were always taking some sort of pet over matters that were entirely unimportant and declaring one of their own sex beyond the pale. Still, he was too shrewd to say so aloud. Instead, he chose another approach.

"What did Philip do?" Darton asked derisively. "Dance more than twice with the girl at one ball?"

"I trust your brothers, none of them, would ever forget themselves so far as to do that unless they were betrothed to the lady in question," Athenia replied, smoothing her amber silk skirt. "Nonetheless, I am told his interest in the girl was quite unmistakable."

"Well, what the devil is wrong with that?" Darton demanded. "Time Philip was wed!"

"Past time," Athenia agreed. "If he chose the right girl. It remains to be seen if he has and it is our duty to see her for ourselves and decide if we wish to encourage the match or whether you must exercise your authority as head of the family to forbid it."

George hesitated. He liked the notion of exercising his authority. It was one of the things he liked best about being Lord Darton. On the other hand, this was Philip she was talking about. He had the lowering thought that if he were to try to forbid Philip from doing something he wished, his brother would merely laugh in his face and he had no desire to put that particular fear to the test.

Still, it was evident, looking at Athenia, that she had made up her mind. And it would have been easier for George to envision crossing Philip than it would be to picture himself crossing his wife.

So, in the end, Lord Darton sighed and said mildly, "As you wish, my dear. As you wish. I suppose I had best at least see the girl in question. Very well, you may send our acceptance."

Since Lady Darton had done so some three hours since, she merely nodded and rose to her feet without haste. No need to tell her husband that she had anticipated his agreement. Men did so like to think they made all the decisions in a household, even when they patently did not. And Athenia's mother had been wise enough to teach her to always pander to this weakness.

Had Emily had any notion what was in store for her, she would have had no hesitation in ripping up the invitation to Lady Jersey's ball. And she would have cared not a jot what her aunt or father said.

But she did not. All she knew was that Lady Jersey was inclined to be kind to her and that it was said all the *ton* would come to her grand event. Emily wished to speak to Lord Beaumont again and also several other gentlemen whose names she had culled from the papers back home.

To be sure, Papa considered it most unladylike that she had read the papers at all, but how else was she to discover who was speaking for what in the House of Lords or the House of Commons?

So without the least inkling of the disaster ahead, Emily blithely made plans for Lady Jersey's ball. She took great pains with her toilette, recalling Mr. Langford's maxim that more battles could be won this way than by direct confrontation. Indeed no one could have found anything to cavil at in her appearance. From the curls on her head to the dashing green satin ball gown to the tips of her satin slippers, she looked every inch the lady.

Mind you, it did briefly occur to Emily that if she should happen to see Lord Darton at the ball, she ought to try to avoid him. But a moment's reflection had reassured her that even if they came face-to-face he was not likely to pay the slightest heed to her. And that even if he did, it was not likely he would connect the young lady at the ball with the hoyden who had tried to storm White's. And should he realize they were one and the same, even he would surely hesitate to create a scene at a ball.

So having reassured himself on all the salient points, Emily headed off to Lady Jersey's ball with a light heart, accompanied by her jubilant father and a very preoccupied Aunt Agatha.

This was, by far, the grandest event to which Emily had received an invitation. She was not prepared, therefore, for the length of time it required before their carriage could reach the door to let them down. Nor was she prepared for the number of linkboys and footmen and other assorted persons keeping order.

Of course, it was the number of candles required to light the household to a brilliant glow that captured her father's attention. Emily could hear him calculating in his head the cost of this single night's expenditure for the same.

As for Aunt Agatha, she almost drew back, but then she took a deep breath, tilted her chin high, and with her eyes commanded Emily to do the same.

It was, Emily told herself, an auspicious beginning for what she began to suspect would be a magical night.

A pity Emily was so poor at prognostication!

Chapter 16

Philip stepped inside the doorway at Lady Jersey's household and immediately realized it had been a mistake not to accompany the Ashbourne party. He would never find them in this crush! Or so he feared. But given how swiftly gossip of his interest in Miss Ashbourne had somehow spread, he had thought it prudent to arrive separately.

He paid his respects to Lady Jersey, flirting with her just as she most liked, and coaxing from her the information that the Ashbournes were here before him. He refused to satisfy her curiosity about the family but salvaged his credit with her by promising to come by with a particularly salacious piece of gossip later in the week.

Then he set about finding Miss Ashbourne and her aunt with grim determination. There were too many pitfalls for a green girl from the country to leave her here on her own for very long.

He had just started looking when a familiar voice hailed him. "Philip!"

"James."

"George is here."

Three simple words. Enough to send a chill through Philip. He shook it off. What odds did it make to him if his brother chose to come to this affair? So long as George didn't encounter Miss Ashbourne, of course, and he rather thought that she would have the sense to stay out of his brother's way.

A look at James's face ought to have been sufficient to warn Philip he was wrong.

"He's here with Athenia and he is looking for your Miss Ashbourne," James said in a low voice.

"Why?"

"Because, dear brother," James said with a mixture of affection and exasperation in his voice, "apparently George and Athenia have heard rumors that some female, by the name of Miss Ashbourne, has you in her clutches and they have come to see if she is a suitable bride for a Langford."

Philip went very pale. "How long have they been here?" he asked. "And have they found her yet?"

James shook his head. "I haven't the faintest notion since I don't know what she looks like either."

He paused, then added, a mischievous note to his voice, "Nor does George seem to realize that this Miss Ashbourne is the same one he had thrown in Bedlam. I shall give a great deal to see his face when he does."

Philip didn't wait to hear any more. He began moving through the crowd, looking for Miss Ashbourne or Miss Jarrod or Mr. Ashbourne. His height, which was above average, gave him some advantage, but not enough. And to his irritation, he realized James was following him.

"What the devil do you think you're doing?" Philip turned and asked his brother.

James grinned unrepentantly. "I want to see what happens when you all meet up together. Besides, I need to tell you about Harry."

That stopped Philip. He looked swiftly around then said in an undervoice, "What about Harry?"

James also glanced swiftly about and pitched his voice low so that only Philip could hear. "He said to tell you he will meet you at your town house after Lady Jersey's ball.

He also told me," he added as Philip turned to head for the door, "to tell you to stay as long as you would if you didn't know he was in town. He says it's important that you do so. No one is to know he is back. Not yet, at any rate."

Philip nodded. His first impulse was to rush straight home. But if Harry said it was important that he not do so, he surely had a good and sufficient reason. In any event, there was still the question of what would happen when his brother found Miss Ashbourne and realized who she was. And, perhaps even more serious, when she realized that Lord Darton was his brother.

The image conjured up by such a disastrous circumstance was sufficient to cause Philip to redouble his efforts to find her.

Lord Darton did not often attend balls. He was scarcely dangling for a wife, having Athenia already. And his children were not yet of an age to require that he take them about to such things. So it was with gratifying warmth that he was greeted by acquaintances as he moved about Lady Jersey's ballroom.

It took, therefore, longer than expected to discover the whereabouts of the unknown Miss Ashbourne. The name nagged at him and he had the feeling he ought to know it. But if so, he could not recall the circumstances.

It was not that the affair with the deranged girl had slipped his mind, precisely, but even at the time he had paid very little attention to who she claimed to be and rather more to how he could be rid of her. So it was not until he was face-to-face with the girl that he realized the enormity of the disaster in which he found himself.

Not that he believed Philip to have a romantic interest in the girl. He discarded that notion the moment he realized who she was. Obviously Athenia had gotten matters all wrong!

No, George was certain Miss Ashbourne must somehow

be a client of Philip's and now he recalled the way his brother had rushed off straightway after he told him the story of having the girl carted off to Bedlam. The devil take it, why must his brother take every stray creature under his wing, anyway?

By his side, Athenia was greeting Miss Ashbourne and her companion. To George's surprise, the older woman's name was familiar to his wife.

"Miss Jarrod? How do you do. I am Lady Darton. I believe my mother once knew you. She was then Corinda Matthews."

"Yes, of course I remember Corinda!" the older woman said with a cry of delight. "And so you are her daughter? May I present my niece, Miss Emily Ashbourne?"

"How do you do," Athenia said graciously.

George knew, however, that her sharp eyes would miss nothing of the girl's appearance. What would she say when he told her this was the girl he had had thrown into Bedlam? The very thought made him shudder. Perhaps Miss Ashbourne wouldn't remember?

And to make matters worse, Sir Thomas Levenger was standing beside Miss Jarrod and appeared to be acquainted with her as well. It only wanted that! Let him get wind of what George had done and the elder man was likely to ring a peal over his head. Sir Thomas seemed to forget that Darton had long since reached his majority and had no need of Levenger's oversight.

If only he hadn't had the girl taken off to Bedlam! But he'd been so sure she was mad. And not really a lady. What lady would have behaved as she did, or spouted such absurd nonsense? It wasn't his fault, surely, that he had mistaken the situation. And perhaps, he thought again, she wouldn't remember.

It was a forlorn hope. Already Athenia was turning toward him and saying, "I must make you both known to my husband, Lord Darton."

He bowed, they curtsied. Miss Ashbourne's eyes widened first in disbelief, then narrowed in suspicion. Darton's only consolation was that matters couldn't get much worse. Except, of course, that they did. His first intimation of just how bad they were going to be was when Athenia said, "Ah, Miss Ashbourne, here are two of my husband's brothers: Mr. James Langford and Mr. Philip Langford."

With a sinking sensation, Darton noted the way Philip greeted Miss Ashbourne, with every evidence of familiarity. And James had that glint in his eye which was enough to tell George that he, too, knew this was the girl who had been carted off to Bedlam. Both turned to regard him quizzically and he realized they did not mean to make matters easy for him. Indeed they were likely to revel in his discomfiture.

Only Sir Thomas was regarding him merely with mild curiosity. But already his shrewd eyes were taking note of how the others were looking at George and he was no doubt drawing his own conclusions.

Abruptly George decided to go on the offensive. He was the head of the family and they ought to respect that fact. He would not apologize for what he had done, but rather expect Philip to apologize for becoming involved with a young lady who could only be trouble.

Or rather, he would have gone on the offensive had Miss Ashbourne not done so first. She was regarding Philip with a grim look on her face. Through clenched teeth she said, "Is this your brother? How odd that you never said a word to the point when you must know I had an interest in Lord Darton's role in the House of Lords."

Philip colored up nicely and George might have permitted himself to enjoy his brother's discomfort if Athenia had not hissed to him, "An interest in the House of Lords? Why, my dear Miss Ashbourne, whatever could you mean? It is hardly the place of a young lady to be concerned with such things."

Emily did not even try to hide her contempt. "Nonetheless, I am," she said. "As Lord Darton is aware."

Athenia looked at her husband, affronted. "What is she talking about? How do you know her, George?"

There was no time to explain. Not in detail. Not with so many people around. As it was, they were beginning to attract attention.

George did the only thing he could think of. He gave James a little nudge and said, "Why don't you ask Miss Ashbourne to dance?"

James glared at him, but his manners, at least, were too good to permit him to refuse to ask the girl. He bowed, she hesitated, then allowed him to lead her away. That left Athenia and Philip both regarding George with expressions of displeasure on their faces. Sir Thomas and Miss Jarrod were even worse. They both looked as if they were about to read him a scold. Perhaps Sir Thomas knew more than he thought, after all.

Hastily, Darton said, "Perhaps we ought to take a turn about the room, Philip? Athenia? Getting deuced warm in here!"

That recollected everyone, as George hoped it would, to the interested ears all about. After a moment Athenia nodded and placed her hand on his arm.

"As usual," she said with creditable calm, "you are right."

Philip took a moment longer, then he, too, nodded curtly and said, "A turn about the room would be an excellent notion."

"Yes, a turn about the room would be an excellent notion," Sir Thomas said with great meaning in his voice. "I've no doubt you have a great many things to talk about. And I wish to dance with Miss Jarrod."

George was actually rather impressed that his impetuous brother managed to make it three-quarters of the way around the room, smiling and nodding to acquaintances, before he gave way to his temper.

"What the devil were you doing, troubling Miss Ashbourne again?" Philip demanded.

"Again?" Athenia echoed.

"Bedlam," George told his wife succinctly.

Athenia was not a stupid woman. Indeed, she prided herself on her understanding, though she was not so unfeminine as to aspire to the title of bluestocking. She grasped what he meant. And, as always, came to his defense. She rounded on Philip, though softly and careful not to draw the attention of those nearby.

"How dare you, sir, consort with a female so likely to embroil us in scandal? How dare you consort with a woman who must be locked up to protect her from herself?"

Athenia did have a tendency to press matters too far, George thought with an inward shudder, and this was one of those times. If he did not say something quickly, Philip was likely to enact a scene and not care a farthing who overheard what.

"I collect I was mistaken in the matter of her wits?" George said before Philip could give way to his rage.

That stopped the barrister, as George knew it would. He opened and closed his mouth several times, even as Athenia pinched Darton's arm. George ignored her and waited for Philip to speak.

Finally Philip said, "Yes, you were mistaken."

George allowed himself to sigh out loud. "I thought so. Pity. Ought to apologize to the girl."

"Yes, you should," Philip agreed, beginning to relax.

George went in for the kill. "I shall apologize to Miss Ashbourne," he said softly, "if you will apologize for so far forgetting what is due your family that you allow your name to be linked with hers! No, don't interrupt. I have agreed she did not belong in Bedlam. But that does not mean I wish to have her name linked with ours. Mad or not, her behavior outside of White's was completely unacceptable, far outside the boundaries of what is right and proper for a lady.

Whether she is a hoyden or worse, her name ought not to be linked with ours. And I tell you frankly, they are laying bets as to whether you will marry her!"

Philip went white then red then white again. Finally, when George stopped speaking, he took his turn. He could not, after all, resist the opportunity with which his brother had presented him.

In a cold, calm voice that was more convincing than any shouting would have been, he said, "I am betrothed to Miss Ashbourne, though we have not yet made it public knowledge, and I suggest you begin to accustom yourself to the notion. I tell you right now that I will not tolerate any disrespect of the lady. Not now, not ever."

Then, before George could collect his wits and remonstrate further, Philip turned on his heel and walked away. He retained sufficient presence of mind to ask a young lady at random to dance, but George would have wagered he didn't even see her face or know with whom he was speaking.

With a sinking sense of dread, he realized his brother was smitten even worse than he feared. By his side, Athenia agreed.

"We must detach him from her. I shan't say it will be easy, for it is clear he has a *tendre* for the girl. Most unsuitable, but there it is. Your brother has always been a difficult man. No sense of what is due his position, or yours. I often fear he has inherited your father's instability of character. You must know I had great difficulty persuading my father that you had not done so. Well, I shall simply have to set to work at once to make him, to make both of them realize the impossibility of such a match."

Those words were sufficient to set a chill in Lord Darton's soul. But he did not dare remonstrate with Athenia. His wife was a formidable woman. Just how formidable he had not realized until it was too late to draw back. And most of the time, if he were honest, George was glad she was.

But tonight her words frightened him. He only wished he could believe they would have the power to frighten Philip.

Chapter 17

Philip was grateful, when he left Sally Jersey's ball, that he had a purpose to going home. He had had very little chance to speak with Miss Ashbourne further. She had made certain of that. He knew she was angry with him and wished she would give him the chance to explain. But she had not. He would have fretted much more had he not had Harry on his mind.

The town house was dark, with only a few candles lit to welcome him back, just as he preferred it to be. So there was no indication, nothing to tell him whether Harry really was here or not.

But James had said he would be, and James was seldom wrong. About anything. Well, it would be just like Harry to prefer secrecy.

Philip entered his house and behaved precisely as he would if he thought no one were there. Just as Harry's instructions, conveyed by way of James, had said he should. He relinquished his hat and gloves and cloak to the one footman waiting up for him and proceeded upstairs. He allowed his valet to partially undress him and he then put on a dressing gown. Finally he padded back downstairs and into the library, as though he had a desire to find something to read.

And there, just as he expected, Philip found Harry waiting for him in the dark, the room lit only by the remains of the carefully banked fire that had all but died out this cool spring night.

Carefully Philip closed the door behind him and came forward into the room, lighting candles as he went.

"Not too many," Harry cautioned.

"No one can see in these windows, particularly not with the draperies drawn," Philip scoffed.

"Yes, but would you light so many candles just for yourself?" Harry demanded. "Or will the servants wonder in the morning?"

Philip hesitated, then nodded and blew out half of those he had already lit and chose with care the few remaining ones he would have used had he been in the library alone.

When both he and Harry were satisfied, the two brothers embraced. Then they stepped back and took chairs facing one another.

"Why the need for such secrecy?" Philip asked.

Harry shrugged and turned his hand one way, then the other. Which meant he either could not or would not answer. Philip leaned back, knowing Harry would explain what he could in his own time and there was no point in trying to rush his brother. Besides, even in this dim light he could see that Harry looked exhausted.

"It looks as if there have been some horrible battles, of late," Philip said quietly.

Harry regarded his brother with a bleak look in his eyes. "The worst, so far, that I've seen. Too many of my friends have died, Philip. And the devil is, we think it was because someone is giving information to the enemy."

Philip drew in a deep breath. "Is that why you're back home? Trying to find out about the spy? Is that why you asked me to find out about a man named Canfield?"

"Have you?" The words came quickly, eagerly.

"A little. Nothing that would help you. But he was betrothed to a lady I know. What do you need me to find out? Or are you here to investigate him yourself?"

Harry shook his head. "I wish I was. No, I'm little more than a glorified messenger boy. But a trusted one and that's more than can be said about some. Still, Canfield might become suspicious if I were to ask questions about him or his mills or try to inspect one."

Philip had a fairly strong notion that his brother's modest assessment of himself greatly understated the matter, but he did not challenge it. Instead he said, "Tell me what I can do to help."

"I should like you to visit Canfield's mills and look for certain things I shall tell you about in a moment. I have yet to think of a plausible reason, but between us we should be able to come up with something," Harry replied with a frown.

Philip's eyes narrowed, "You may safely leave that to me," he said. "I think I know how the trick might be done."

It was a measure of the trust between the brothers that Harry did not doubt Philip's word. He merely nodded.

"What is it you wish me to look for?" Philip persisted.

Harry leaned forward and in a few words explained as much as he could. "We think someone is supplying the French with our uniforms so that their spies can pass undetected through our lines."

"Couldn't they just be stealing uniforms? From prisoners? Or even dead men?" Philip asked with a frown.

Harry hesitated. "We have reason to believe the uniforms they wear are new. And we think Canfield is supplying them to the French."

Philip drew in his breath with an audible sound.

"Just so," Harry agreed. "And the military has agreed to pretend to order new uniforms from Canfield to see if he ships some to the French."

"And then let the French use them and no one else so you can spot the spies easily?" Philip suggested.

Harry grimaced. "You would think so. But the order was placed and now those in charge have said they intend to actually have our men use the uniforms as well, rather than let them go to waste. And because they fear that if there is some leak elsewhere in the ministry, the French will be warned off. So unless we intercept the entire shipment, some spies will use them and slip through our lines unsuspected. But it's my friends and I who will die because of bureaucratic obstinacy! A pity there's no way to mark the uniforms that will get through, but they will not even give me approval to try."

Harry paused and seemed to make an effort to collect himself. Finally he said, "What I should like is for you to find an excuse, if you can, to travel into the countryside to visit Canfield's mills. See if you can discover the route by which he passes the uniforms to the smugglers who will take them to the French. But be careful! And above all, give Canfield no hint of what you are about."

Philip nodded his comprehension. "I understand. But what are we to say when asked why you are here in London?"

"No one is to know any message has been sent back here," Harry answered slowly, "so no one must know or guess that that is the purpose of my visit. Or that we mean to find out about Canfield. When I publicly arrive, tomorrow, it will be because my oldest brother has summoned me home to deal with a family crisis. You."

"Me?" Philip echoed, taken aback.

Harry grinned. "Yes, you. It seems you've taken up with a most unlikely creature and if we don't all take a hand to stop you, you'll bring shame down upon the family. Now since I must suppose that you have already, publicly no doubt, flaunted the creature before George, no one will doubt my story. Particularly not if you pretend to be serious about the girl and George continues to make clear his displeasure in the possible match."

Philip frowned and shook his head slowly. "You've spoken to George already? But I would have sworn he didn't know, before tonight, that she was the same girl he had thrown into Bedlam."

Harry gave a tiny crow of laughter. "I knew I was right! The rumor mill was not mistaken. You are involved with a most ineligible creature! And George does disapprove. And I'll wager you all but came to blows tonight, in public!"

Philip merely glared at his brother and, after a moment, Harry said, "I have not yet spoken to George but I shall ask him to pretend he sent for me because he was worried about you. With George, there is no need to tell him anything more. He will play his part well enough without any prodding from me."

"And how am I supposed to respond to your presence in London?" Philip asked dryly.

Harry waved a careless hand. "You resent it. You resent my interference and George for requesting it. I, of course, pay no attention to your disapproval. Together we shall contrive to drive you out of London. And while you are in the country, perhaps you can find the chance to visit Canfield's mill. Between us, we shall give the gossipmongers such a show that no one will think to wonder at how long or short I stay. And when I am ready to return to the front lines, why, we shall come to terms and I shall gracefully withdraw, satisfied that I have made you come to your senses."

"And if you have not?" Philip asked softly.

Harry's eyes widened. "Do you mean you are serious about the girl?" he asked in astonishment.

"I don't know," Philip replied irritably, rising to his feet and beginning to pace about the room. "This girl, as you call her, is the one who was betrothed to Canfield. I shall make an excuse to escort her to her home and let her show me his mills. She is, you see, an ardent reformer. I shall let her think she is beginning to persuade me around to her point of view."

"Famous! It will answer perfectly," Harry said with a note of awe in his voice.

Philip paused in his pacing and frowned. "I am not so sure. I do not like making Miss Ashbourne such an object of conjecture. I have done more of that than I like already. Nor do I wish to place her in any danger. Perhaps I ought not to involve her."

"Well, I cannot answer that question for you," Harry said dryly, "but at least I now know that your heart is clearly engaged."

"And if it is?" Philip challenged.

Harry hesitated, then shrugged. "The devil's in it, then. I thought the girl was merely a means to annoy George, but patently she is not. Well, I suppose I shall have to either pretend I have found Miss Ashbourne acceptable or decided to gracefully retire from the lists, having persuaded myself there is nothing I can do to dissuade you from your disastrous course. Either way, it will suffice and no one will be the wiser as to my true purpose in being here, in London."

"Including me, I suppose," Philip said wryly. "No, don't bother to try to gammon me with any more tales. I shan't ask you any more questions and you shan't have to tell me any more lies. It is enough to have you here, to know you are safe, and to have a little time with you before you must go back. And yes, much as I dislike it, I shall use Miss Ashbourne as a ruse to visit Canfield's mills but I shall make certain that he does not blame her if anything should go wrong."

"I knew I could count on you!"

Harry smiled and a message of affection passed between them, conveyed more eloquently by the way they looked at one another than words could ever have done. Then Harry rose to his feet.

"I'd best be on my way," he said. "I must ride back to an inn outside of London so that tomorrow I can make my grand entrance home."

Philip nodded and rose to his feet. "I'll show you out," he said.

Harry shook his head. "No need. The window will suffice. And less chance of meeting anyone in the hallway. Just help me blow out the candles first. I shouldn't want anyone watching to see me lit from behind."

Moments later he was gone. Philip silently closed the window behind him, looked about the room to make certain nothing betrayed the fact that Harry had been there at all, then he seized a book, almost at random, and left the room.

Chapter 18

Emily was shaken. How, she wondered, does one get past such deceit as this? Why had Mr. Langford not told her that Lord Darton was his brother? Why had Sir Thomas not told her of the connection between her uncle's friend and the barrister to whom he sent her?

When asked, Sir Thomas had shrugged, pasted a vague look on his face which she did not believe, waved his hand carelessly, and said that it must have slipped his mind. Just as it must have slipped Mr. Langford's mind, no doubt, that he had not told her, after he rescued her from Bedlam, about the connection between himself and Lord Darton. It was most distressing.

What also worried Emily was that she found it difficult to believe that Mr. Langford could truly support her if he was Lord Darton's brother. His lordship had not granted her much time to speak, or he to reply, before calling for someone to take her away to Bedlam. But that short time had been sufficient for him to make clear his views. And they did not include even the smallest possibility of support for such reforms as Emily wished to champion.

Still, she did not hold the same views as her father, so it was at least possible that Mr. Langford and his brother disagreed. The other brother seemed to think so. If only she could know for certain. Having made a mistake in putting her trust in one man, Emily had no intention of doing so a second time.

Sleep did not come easily, after they returned home that evening. Dawn found her still tossing and turning and reluctantly she rose to face the day.

At least Papa was pleased. The morning after Lady Jersey's ball he positively rubbed his hands together with glee as he said, "Lord and Lady Darton distinguishing you with their notice! Splendid, absolutely splendid. And reminding, thereby, everyone of Mr. Langford's excellent connections. I begin to think you have done very well for yourself, Emily. Very well, indeed. Now you mustn't be missish about the matter. You need a husband. There is only one more point to resolve, the question of how generous a settlement Mr. Langford is willing to make. What are his finances? Excellent, I suppose. They must be for him to live at the address he does. Well, you must find out. Or I will, should the opportunity present itself. Agatha, it is a great pity you didn't think to ask his brother."

"What reason could I possibly have given for such effrontery?" Miss Jarrod gasped.

Ashbourne waved a hand. "I don't know. You should have thought of something. Ah, well, I shall just have to do it myself."

But Emily had finally found her voice. "You wouldn't, Papa! You cannot mean to shame us this way."

"Shame you? Nonsense! It is merely being practical and let me tell you that if you think other fathers don't inquire into the state of finances of suitors for their daughters, well, you very much mistake the matter! A fine thing it would be if I didn't care whether the fellow could support my daughter or not."

Ashbourne managed to sound greatly aggrieved. Emily did not bother to answer. She knew only too well that her father was less concerned with Mr. Langford's ability to support her than with whether he could wring sufficient sterling from the man to fund his stables.

Instead, she turned and stared once more out the window.

Not that there was any great view from an address such as theirs, but it was better than looking at her father chortle over what he called her good fortune or her aunt smile secretly over some happy thoughts of her own. Thoughts that Emily was willing to wager included Sir Thomas Levenger.

Emily wished her aunt happy, she truly did, but it hurt to think that Aunt Agatha had a better chance at happiness than she did. Mr. Langford had never looked at her with the sort of admiration and affection that shone so patently in Sir Thomas Levenger's face when he looked at Aunt Agatha. No, the most she could expect from Mr. Langford was that he had somehow conceived he had a responsibility for her welfare.

Intent as she was on the view from the window, Emily still did not see Mr. Langford arrive. She all but jumped when his name was announced and he entered. His eyes flew to her face and she could only lower her gaze, as swiftly as possible, to the floor before she betrayed herself.

"Hallo, Langford," her father said, striding forward to shake his hand.

He murmured something Emily could not quite hear. Then she felt, rather than saw him turn to Aunt Agatha. As always, his kindness to her aunt warmed Emily's heart. How could she not like such a man? He even teased Aunt Agatha about Sir Thomas Levenger and managed to surprise a little laugh out of her. And for that, Emily would have forgiven him much. She could even, almost, forgive him for not telling her that Lord Darton was his brother.

And then Mr. Langford was looking at her. It was as if there was an apology, and something else she could not comprehend, in his eyes.

"I came to ask," he said gruffly, "if you would care to go for a drive with me, Miss Ashbourne."

Something in the way he asked, in the way he stood, conveyed to her how important it was to him, this most conventional of requests. She hesitated only a moment.

"Of course," she said lightly. "If you will give me five minutes to get ready?"

He bowed. She retreated. And hastened to her room. She would not keep him waiting, not when her father meant to subject him to a quizzing. A quick repinning of her hair, a hasty smoothing of her blue cloth skirt and donning a darker blue pelisse, a moment to pinch her cheeks, and one or two other little matters and she was hurrying back down the stairs. Even so, she had taken longer than was wise.

"A tidy sum," she heard her father saying thoughtfully. "Not excessive, mind, but sufficient for you to support a household and be beforehand with the world even if you choose to indulge in a few luxuries. Tell me, sir, have you ever considered investing in horses?"

"I am ready!" Emily cried, diverting attention from her father.

They all looked at her strangely and she colored up but she would not apologize for rescuing Mr. Langford from her father's efforts to importune him for money. He quirked an eye but merely offered her his arm and together they retreated to the street where a carriage waited and a groom was standing at the horses' heads.

Emily tilted her head to look up at Mr. Langford. "Another brother's carriage and groom?" she asked.

To her surprise, he reddened and said, an unexpected stiffness to his voice, "No, it is mine. I thought it about time I set up my own stable instead of always borrowing from James. Or even George."

And more, Emily could see, he was not likely to say. It was odd, but only one more odd thing about this man and not, in her view, the most important. And then she forgot all about the new carriage, for her thoughts were on the man himself. It wasn't sensible, it wasn't prudent, but Emily felt a surge of pleasure as Mr. Langford handed her to her seat.

And it was the oddest thing. With each street corner they passed, his mood seemed to lighten as well and he began to actually smile. But he did not speak until they reached the park. Then he pulled the carriage up short and handed the reins to the groom.

This was, she thought, becoming a distinct habit with the man. Still, she had a few things she wished to say to him and without being overheard so she was pleased, rather than otherwise, when he said, "Miss Ashbourne, would you care to take a turn on foot?"

It was not really a question. Once again his eyes asked her to agree and curiosity, if nothing else, would have compelled her to do so. Only when they were some distance down the path did he explain.

"I am sorry to drag you about this way," he said by way of beginning, "but I needed to speak to you in private, where we would not be overheard, and could think of no other way to do so without it looking very particular."

"A very good notion," she said approvingly. "For I have wanted the chance to thank you for protecting me with this pretend betrothal. And to apologize for being angry with you last night. I have come to see that you owed me no explanation about your brother."

This last was said with some difficulty and caused the corners of Mr. Langford's mouth to turn up with amusement. "Someone has taught you excellent manners, Miss Ashbourne," he said, "even if I suspect you would still like to rip up at me over the question of Lord Darton! I do apologize. But I never mentioned him because I knew beforehand he would not aid your cause and afterwards, well, what can one say when one has a relative who puts one to the blush in such a way?"

Now it was Emily's turn to smile. And she did not want to do so. She bit her lower lip to keep from grinning outright. Still, there was a question she could not resist asking. "How did Lord Darton turn out so different from your father? And you? Only your brother James seems in the least like the man I met once at my uncle's house, years ago."

Suddenly the humor was gone from his eyes and they turned very dark. Emily shivered, though it was in truth a very warm day. Mr. Langford's voice, when it came, only chilled her even more.

"My father was a romantic. An idealist. And a trouble-maker. Oh, yes, he liked to cause trouble and then stand back and watch. He did good, I suppose. I'll grant you that. But it cost us, his family, a great deal. He alienated almost every friend my parents had ever had. George was the eldest and he felt it even more than I. James was too young to understand much of what was happening or to be affected by it but George and Harry and I were not."

Emily put a hand on his arm. Gently she said, "I am very sorry he caused you and your family so much grief."

He looked down at her and there was not a shred of warmth in his eyes now as he said, "But you are not sorry he was the man he was."

It was a question and Emily could not pretend it wasn't. Nor could she lie. "No," she said, her voice still soft, "I cannot regret the man your father was. Not when I recall the admiration with which my uncle always spoke of him."

He drew in a deep breath and then nodded curtly. "That, more than anything else, Miss Ashbourne," he said, "explains the deep gulf between us!"

He stared down at her hand and she slowly let go of his arm. With a composure she was far from feeling, Emily said, "You need not fear, Mr. Langford, that I shall mistake your kindness for anything more. Nor try to hold you to this betrothal you are pretending to for my sake. The moment I have secured some sort of position, on my own, I shall release you. You may be certain of that. Indeed, if you wish, I shall go home today and tell my father that it is at an end and let him take me to be a governess with the family he spoke of. I only beg that if I do so you will help Aunt Agatha travel to whichever family member she seeks shelter from."

Abruptly he cursed and all the stiffness went out of his

body. There was a haunted look in his eyes as he said, "No! Miss Ashbourne, I did not mean for you to take it so! Indeed, there is a favor I brought you here to ask."

He paused and did not seem to know quite how to continue. He took a deep breath, then plunged in as though otherwise he might lose his nerve.

"Miss Ashbourne, could you, would you, allow yourself to pretend to be routed from London, on some pretext? Perhaps by Lady Darton? I have no doubt she will try to drive you away and I should like you to allow yourself to be persuaded to leave London. And I should like you to let me accompany you when you go."

Emily blinked. Whatever she had been expecting, it was not this. He wanted to visit her home? Why? A part of her leaped in happiness, thinking that perhaps it meant he had a *tendre* for her after all.

A more sensible part of her viewed Mr. Langford's request with the greatest suspicion. She did not believe that he had suddenly conceived a grand passion for her. And if he had, it would not explain why he wished to leave London. Something was very strange here.

"I am willing to do so," she said slowly, when she finally answered him, "and to have you come with me. But may I ask why you wish to do so?"

"I cannot tell you."

Well, that was a facer. And it did not improve her temper. Emily was tempted to tell him precisely what she thought of such high-handedness.

But she didn't. There was something about the way he stood, the way he looked at her, that conveyed, more clearly than words could have done, how important this was to Mr. Langford. And Emily found herself trusting him.

"Very well," she said. "When do you wish to leave London?"

"As soon as possible. And, Miss Ashbourne, there is more."

"More?"

"I wish to visit Mr. Canfield's mills while we are there."

Emily felt a blinding flash of revelation. She reached out and clasped his hand. It was most improper, most forward, but she could not help herself, any more than she could help the look of joy that came into her eyes.

"Truly? Do you mean it? Of course I shall allow myself to be routed! Oh course I shall take you to see Mr. Canfield's mills! Why should you think, how could you think, that I would possibly object to seeing you finally begin to follow in your father's footsteps?"

That he looked most uncomfortable, Emily allowed herself to pretend she did not see. Instead she dwelt on the fact that finally Mr. Langford was willing to observe the situation for himself firsthand. Surely, once he did so, he would be wholeheartedly on her side.

So she was all affability as they returned to Mr. Langford's carriage and tooled about the park for a short while. What did it matter what excuse he used? He wanted to see Mr. Canfield's mills and that, Emily thought blissfully, was all that mattered.

Chapter 19

Athenia, Lady Darton, was not content to let matters rest. While Miss Ashbourne was not entirely unsuitable, it was clear to her that Philip could do much better for himself and it was her duty to make certain he did so. She knew what he owed his family, even if he did not!

Her first decision was to call upon Miss Ashbourne. She had seemed a sensible girl and not altogether pleased with Philip in the first place. If she could be persuaded to relinquish her pretensions, all would be well.

Unfortunately, Athenia arrived in front of the town house hired by the Ashbournes just as Philip and the girl returned from a drive. She was laughing as Philip handed her down and neither noticed Athenia. It was a circumstance that did not improve her disposition.

"Hello, Miss Ashbourne," she said, a trifle shrilly. "And Philip. You appear to have had a satisfactory outing."

If her manner was meant to overwhelm Miss Ashbourne, it succeeded. Instantly the laughter was gone from the girl's face and she went pale. Good! Next Athenia turned her attention to Philip and was dismayed to see that far from being abashed, he brazenly slipped an arm around the girl's waist and grinned defiantly at his sister-in-law.

"Come to meet my fiancèe, have you?" he asked.

Athenia felt her mouth gape open. Philip had said something of the sort the night before, but surely he had been roasting them? Surely matters had not truly gone so far? Hastily she shut it.

"Fiancèe?" she echoed. Then, recollecting herself, she drew herself to her full height and said condescendingly, "I have never liked such humor, Philip. It is not at all kind to the girl in question."

He lifted his eyebrows at her. "Unkind to make you known to her before the announcement is sent to the papers?"

Dear God, he was serious! But perhaps the matter was not entirely beyond salvaging. After all, he said the notice had not yet been sent.

Athenia permitted herself a thin smile. "Do give over jesting, Philip. Miss Ashbourne is far too wise to agree to marry you."

Something flashed in Miss Ashbourne's eyes, something that gave Athenia a distinct sense of unease. It worsened as the girl said, "Am I?"

But Athenia was not easily daunted. She rallied. "Of course you are."

"Why?"

"I beg your pardon?"

"Why would it be unwise of me to marry Mr. Langford?"

The girl was pert and impertinent and altogether impossible! Athenia's face took on a pinched expression as she said, "You must see it would not do! The two of you are not in the least suitable for one another. You need a country squire or something of the sort, someone entirely conventional, Miss Ashbourne. Philip equally needs someone entirely conventional. Why, if the two of you married, as unconventional as you both are, it would be impossible! You would put yourselves beyond the pale."

They did not at once answer and she pressed her advantage. "Mind you, there is also the question of money. A vulgar subject, I will allow, but Philip really should make a push to marry an heiress. And considering the location of the house which you hired, Miss Ashbourne, I think I may safely judge that you would do well to marry someone far better circumstanced than Philip. Perhaps even a wealthy merchant would do for you."

Once again they did not answer her and Athenia congratulated herself on hitting on precisely the right manner in which to approach the pair. She began to think she had resolved the matter entirely.

Until Philip spoke, that is. The instant he opened his mouth and she heard his first words, Athenia knew there would be trouble.

"My dear sister-in-law, how sweet of you to take such an interest in my affairs," Philip said, "but I am not quite a pauper. Money need not be my primary reason to marry. But in any event, I do wish you would not make a present of your thoughts to the entire street. Do you not think it would be better to go inside and talk there? That is, if Miss Ashbourne is willing to extend to you the courtesy of her house after your words to her."

"Yes, of course I am," Miss Ashbourne said instantly.

She smiled at Athenia, who did not wish to be smiled at. It would have been better had the girl taken a pet. As it was, Athenia, who prided herself on her grasp of propriety, appeared to be the vulgar one.

With poor humor, Athenia followed the pair into the dingy house that did nothing to exceed her expectations. To be sure, Miss Jarrod was presentable—after all she knew Athenia's mother—and Mr. Ashbourne was unquestionably a gentleman, but the manner in which he oozed affability could only set her teeth on edge.

Nor was there any way to graciously decline a discussion of her mother. And yet Athenia could not possibly imagine what might ever have drawn the two women together.

And there was no way to prevent Philip from drawing Miss Ashbourne aside to chat with her privately. Not when

Mr. Ashbourne hovered about, joining in her conversation and refusing to care what his daughter did.

Athenia felt nothing so much as a profound sense of frustration and failure as she rose to leave the house. She would not, she decided, inform George of what she had intended. He was far too likely to twit her for her lack of success than to applaud the effort.

And then, suddenly, all fell into place precisely as Athenia wished. Miss Ashbourne turned a soulful gaze toward Lady Darton and said almost tearfully, "Do you truly think it would ruin Mr. Langford if I married him?"

"Inevitably!" Athenia said, disregarding the gasps of outrage by Miss Jarrod and Mr. Ashbourne. "You are nothing like the sort of wife he needs."

"How dare you talk to my daughter in such a way?" Mr. Ashbourne thundered.

"How dare you talk to my fiancèe in such a way?" Philip echoed.

"Really, Lady Darton, I think Corinda must have taught you better manners than that!" Miss Jarrod protested.

Philip put an arm around Miss Ashbourne. She shook it off and pulled away from him. She even dabbed a handkerchief at the corner of her eyes.

"Oh, Papa, Aunt Agatha, I cannot think! It is all so very distressing. I cannot give Mr. Langford up and yet I do not wish to ruin him. I am so very confused! I wish to return home at once!" she said.

And then, even as everyone began to protest again, Miss Ashbourne fled the room. Athenia braved the storm of protest that broke over her head. It was not easy, but she knew her duty and bore it well.

Finally, when the clamor began to subside, she said, rising to her feet with dignity, "You are all overset and it is not to be wondered at. I shall take my leave. Please understand that I have done what I believe best both for Philip and for

Miss Ashbourne. I wish her well, but with a husband better
suited to her than my husband's brother."

Then, well satisfied, if a trifle overwhelmed herself at the
success of her mission, Athenia left the Ashbourne household. She did not see Miss Ashbourne watching her from an
upstairs window nor guess that the moment she was gone,
the girl rushed back downstairs to speak again with Philip.

Had she only know it, Lady Darton's efforts fit in per-
fectly with Harry Langford's plans. He arrived in front of
Lord Darton's town house just as Athenia was leaving Miss
Ashbourne's lodgings.

Harry made something of a production of having his baggage unloaded. The front door was open well before he had
mounted the steps to rap on it. Within moments, several
footmen appeared to carry his luggage in and still Harry
took his time paying off the coachman and going inside. It
was as if he wished the whole street to take note of his appearance.

Inside he was informed that neither Lord nor Lady Darton
were at home, but both were expected at any time.

"No matter," Harry said airily. "Show me to my room and
let me wash off my travel dirt." When this request produced
an expression of confusion, he frowned. "Did my brother
not tell you to expect me?"

"No, sir."

"Oh, the devil! No doubt he wasn't certain I would be
able to come. And I did not stop to answer him, for by his
letter, I concluded the matter was urgent."

"Matter, sir? Urgent?"

Harry merely looked at the fellow as if the man had spoken out of turn. Which of course he had. Even a trusted family retainer ought to have known better than to overstep his
bounds in such a way. The man colored up and hastily
looked away.

"I shall fetch the housekeeper, sir," he said and went to do so.

The other servants, Harry noted with satisfaction, looked at one another with even more confusion than before. Good. It would cause them to spread the word even quicker.

Despite the absence of Lord and Lady Darton, the household was an efficient one and the housekeeper quickly summoned to decide on a room for Captain Langford. And by the time the master returned, Harry was waiting for his brother in the library.

George seemed very happy to see him. "Harry! What a surprise! What a wonderful surprise! What the devil are you doing here?"

"Why, George," he said in a booming voice as he clasped his brother's hand, "I came at your request!"

Since this was accompanied by a speaking look, George immediately fell in with the scheme. "Oh, yes, yes, of course. Just didn't expect you quite so soon. Wasn't sure when you would get away. Er, remind me, again, why I asked you to come?"

This last was said softly, so that the servants outside the room could not hear. Harry grinned unrepentantly and said, his voice as loud as before, "You seemed so worried about Philip, that I requested leave and came at once."

George frowned and motioned for his brother to take a chair, one well away from the door. "Yes, well, I am concerned," he admitted, "and should be glad of your advice. Philip seems to have entangled himself with a most unsuitable young lady."

"An opera dancer?" Harry hazarded lightly, pretending ignorance.

George shook his head. "Worse. A reformer."

His eyes were dancing but Harry managed to keep his expression sober as he said, "How shocking!"

"You may jest about the matter," George retorted, "but I

tell you the girl is a hoyden! Accosted me outside of White's!"

"Obviously you had best buy her off at once," Harry suggested.

"You cannot buy off a reformer," George snapped. "The only thing they wish to hear is that you mean to fall in with their plans. And heaven help you if you don't. Buy her off? Easier to buy off Philip. And the devil is, he won't listen to me. Especially since I had her thrown into Bedlam."

"You had her thrown into Bedlam?" Harry echoed, his voice betraying a hint of glee.

George shifted uncomfortably. "Yes, well, how was I to know she wasn't mad?"

"How indeed?"

"And the devil is, I can't seem to make Philip see sense!" George added irritably. "Athenia means to try her touch with the girl but I haven't any great hopes in that direction. Not a girl to listen to common sense, I should say."

Harry shrugged. "Perhaps you'd best make up your mind to accept the match, then. Is the girl's background really so impossible?"

"No," George admitted slowly. "Her aunt was even once a bosom bow of Athenia's mother. Until she disgraced herself by almost running off with Sir Thomas Levenger. Before he became respectable. You know that family was never quite the thing! And I fear she has influenced her niece, Miss Ashbourne, the object of Philip's attention. Her breeding is sound, but Miss Ashbourne is a shockingly unconventional girl and we have had enough of that in this family!"

Harry's eyes seemed to dance with amusement. "And Philip is captivated with her? Our brother most sober and conventional, after you? You had best make up your mind to accept the match," he repeated. "But not, I pray you, until after I return to Spain."

George eyed Harry thoughtfully. "Something smoky

going on," he said at last. "And I know you won't tell me what it is so I shan't bother to ask."

"Excellent brother!" Harry said approvingly.

"Yes, well, can you at least tell me how long you mean to be here, in London?"

"I don't know," Harry answered promptly.

"Well, while you are, you may as well make yourself useful and try to make your brother Philip see some sense," George said shortly. "Assuming, that is, that Athenia cannot succeed in prying the girl away from him. She might, there's no saying she won't, for Athenia's a remarkable woman and once she sets her sights on a thing, it's as good as done. But I don't mind telling you I have my doubts this time. The girl is most unusual. Most unusual, indeed. So if Athenia doesn't succeed, you'd best have a go at it."

"Oh, I meant to," Harry said. "No one shall doubt I came to try to dissuade Philip from disaster. Whether he will listen to me or not, however, is another question entirely. Now, tell me, this matter aside, how is Athenia? And how are the children?"

As Harry had known he would, Lord Darton happily settled in to tell his brother about his wondrously intelligent and spirited offspring. And Harry was able to lean back in his chair and relax, knowing that, for the moment, no more questions would be asked of him.

Besides, he liked to know what his nephews were up to. It helped to remind him how fortunate he was that he had no children of his own.

Harry strolled into White's as though he had not a care in the world. Or, rather, as though he were pretending to. His friends noticed that he asked, with some urgency, if any of them had seen his brother Philip. And when Philip, himself, entered the club, Harry was seen to abruptly break away from these friends and stride, with great purpose, to where his brother stood.

"Philip!"

"Harry! What the devil are you doing in London?"

"Come to see you, of course."

"George?"

"Yes, well, on that head, perhaps we ought to speak in private."

"There is no need," Philip countered grimly.

It was as good as a play, both men knowing their lines perfectly. Harry was the epitome of concern, Philip the outraged brother, resenting every hint of criticism of his behavior as the conversation continued.

"Anything you wish to say, you may say here, Harry. Though I tell you frankly, I've no need of your brotherly advice, were you considering offering any."

"Philip, the devil take it, you can't wish me to bandy a lady's name about here, in public."

"I don't wish you to bandy any lady's name about at all. And blast George for his impertinence in saying anything to you about the matter!"

"Come, now, Philip, you must understand his concern. He is our eldest brother, after all."

"That does not give him, or you, the right to attempt to interfere in my life!"

"You surely cannot expect us to merely stand by and watch as you make a fool of yourself," Harry protested.

Philip pushed past his brother, saying, "You must excuse me, Harry, I've friends waiting to see me. And if you are worried, you needn't be. Nor need George. I mean to escort the lady in question back to her home in a day or two and neither of you need watch me, as you say, make a fool of myself over anyone!"

And that was that. The entire club was privy to the manner in which Philip Langford stalked, tight-lipped, to another room. And how he did not speak to his brother again for the entire evening.

As for Captain Harry, more than one of his friends shook

their heads over his preoccupation that made him lose more than was his wont at cards. And they all pretended not to notice as he muttered to himself under his breath.

It was all too fascinating for words and a good many people treasured up what they had seen and heard or been told of, to repeat to friends, or wives, on the morrow.

No one saw, or would have paid any note if they had, Philip arrive on Sir Thomas Levenger's doorstep a short time later. He was admitted at once, as a favored guest, and soon explaining to Sir Thomas precisely what he meant to do and why. He knew that Harry would have given his consent, had he been asked.

And when Philip left, an hour later, he had the advantage of the older man's wisdom and advice. Now he felt prepared for his visit to the country and Canfield's mills. And he also found himself wondering just what sort of adventures Sir Thomas might have had in his salad days!

Chapter 20

Several days later, Philip paused his new carriage some distance from the mill and turned to Emily. "I do not wish to alarm Canfield or have him take action against any of the workers who speak to me," he said. "I shall pretend to be quite reluctant to be at the mill. An utterly frippery fellow."

She nodded, for they had talked of this before. "I understand and ask only that you truly look about you and listen to what the workers say and think how you would feel in their shoes."

It was Philip's turn to nod. He had not and did not intend to tell her that he would also be looking about him for a way to verify Harry's suspicions. And to make contact with someone who would be willing and able to help him prove them. The fewer who knew his purpose the better. And in any event, ignorance would serve to keep Emily, Miss Ashbourne, safe. Or so he hoped.

With a growing sense of unease, Philip set the horses once more on their way toward the mill. He wished he could quash this growing sense of impending disaster.

The mill was noisy and full of fabric dust and busy with workers rushing from one point to another. Canfield surveyed first the mill and then Philip and Emily.

"Why did you say you wished to see my mill?"

Philip yawned while Emily tapped her foot impatiently. "Oh, I promised Miss Ashbourne I would visit," Langford said carelessly. "She would have it that you were in need of a number of improvements but I can't say that I think so. Your workers seem most, er, efficient."

Canfield seemed to swell with pride. "They are," he conceded. "My workers are the top producers in the county. Indeed, I've just managed to get a new contract for uniforms for the military because they know I'll have no problem meeting the deadline they set."

Emily tugged at his sleeve. "You must come talk with some of the workers, Philip!" she said.

He rolled his eyes at Canfield. "Do you mind terribly if we do so?" he asked, almost hopefully.

Canfield seemed to take a malicious satisfaction in waving his hand and saying, "Not at all. First I shall give you a tour and then you may speak to whomever you wish."

"Thank you so much," Philip replied with what seemed to be heavy irony.

Canfield smiled. He did glance at Emily, who pretended to pout. The smile broadened. And he led the way toward the nearest group of workers.

"We make the fabric here and in the next building are my cutters and seamstresses who will make the fabric up into uniforms."

"How fascinating," Philip said in a voice that implied he found the entire matter deadly boring.

"Philip, you promised you would pay attention!" Emily said, pinching at his arm.

Again Canfield and Philip exchanged speaking glances. By the time Canfield had shown them through the mill he seemed satisfied that not only did Philip pose no threat to his interests, but that he himself had had a narrow escape from being leg-shackled to Miss Ashbourne.

"Now may we speak with the workers?" Emily demanded petulantly.

"Really, is it absolutely necessary?" Philip asked in the same bored voice he had so carefully cultivated.

"Please, by all means, speak to whomever you will," Canfield said, grinning spitefully.

With a sigh, Philip allowed himself to be led toward a nearby group of workers. The moment Canfield had left the floor of the mill, however, all of Philip's languid air instantly dropped away, as did Emily's petulance.

The workers nearest the couple formed a circle around them and Emily made the introductions. Philip shook hands with each worker. The questions he asked would have raised a distinct alarm with Canfield had he overheard them.

Emily, meanwhile, found herself surrounded by a number of the women. Philip seized his opportunity to make certain arrangements. By the time he was done, he had a promise that several of the workers would be here to let him into the mill on the following evening.

And then, before Canfield's curiosity or alarm could be raised by too long a delay, Philip and Emily left the mill. Philip was careful to praise the mill, yet again, to Canfield and Emily managed to look as though she were about to burst into tears. Only Canfield looked happy.

When they were well down the road, Emily looked at Philip and said doubtfully, "You didn't mean all those things you said, did you?"

Philip smiled at her and shook his head. "Was I that convincing? Perhaps I ought to take to the stage. What do you think?"

Relieved, she smiled in return. "I think we put Mr. Canfield off the scent, just as you said," she replied. "Conditions truly are dreadful in the mill and the worst of it is that he is so proud of himself and I have no notion how to stop him."

Philip hesitated. Then, slowly, he said, "If there were a way to cause Canfield trouble, do you think the workers would help us?"

"Will the mill be closed? As bad as the conditions are,

they have no other place to work or they would already have gone," she countered.

He had no immediate answer for her. But the justice of her question could not be denied.

"I shall stand warrant that even if Canfield were to lose the mill, I should undertake to buy it and keep it open," Philip said at last.

"Then they will help."

"It is that simple?"

"Yes."

But of course it wasn't. Nothing was simple that day. They had gone not a mile farther down the road when the carriage suddenly lurched to the side and overturned, tumbling Emily and Philip and the groom into a ditch.

Philip looked down at Emily with concern. "Are you all right?" he asked, helping her to her feet.

She was shaky and pale. Her light blue dress and dark blue spencer were slightly the worse for wear and her bonnet was askew, but she nodded. They both turned to survey the damage. One wheel of the carriage lay in the ditch beside the road and the carriage itself was overturned. The horses were struggling in the traces, but the groom was trying feverishly to get them in hand again.

Miss Ashbourne moved to study the carriage closer, but Philip did not bother. What was done was done. The immediate question was what they ought to do next. He tried to think. How far were they from a village? Useless to ask the groom. He asked Miss Ashbourne.

She hesitated, then told him, "We are no more than a mile, I should think, from my father's house." To the groom she added, "We shall send back help as soon as possible."

That gave Philip pause. "Are you certain you wish to walk so far?" he asked. "Perhaps we ought to send the groom and you and I wait here."

She surprised him once again. "I have looked closely at

your carriage, even if you have not, and if the wheel was not tampered with, I should be very much surprised. Someone presumably did not like our visit to Mr. Canfield's mill and I should not like to have them follow and find us helpless here. I should much rather take my chances on foot, across the fields."

The groom made some sound of protest at these words and Miss Ashbourne turned to him and said kindly, "No one would have any reason to harm you. They will presume you know nothing about this. You will be perfectly safe here. It is only Mr. Langford and myself who need worry."

Then catching up her skirt with one hand she leaped over the ditch. "Coming Mr. Langford?" she called back to him.

There was nothing for it, Philip decided, except to do as she wished. He took a moment to give the groom some additional instructions, then leaped over the ditch after her. Miss Ashbourne was not, he thought irritably, a conventional young lady and he was getting very tired of the consequences of that.

But conventional or not, Miss Ashbourne knew the way across the fields and they reached her home sooner than he would have thought possible. She stopped short, however, at the edge of the woods that bounded the house from one side.

He started to ask why, then noted the carriage pulled up before the door. Canfield's carriage. Philip drew in a deep breath. The man had just arrived and was even now striding up the front steps.

"I think," Miss Ashbourne said in a small voice beside him, "that we should perhaps wait until he leaves."

Philip was inclined to agree. Though it went against the grain not to confront the man openly, he had a more important duty to protect Miss Ashbourne. And he had no doubt, that if her suspicions about the wheel were correct, that it would be safer for both of them if Canfield did not at once discover they had returned to Miss Ashbourne's home.

And yet, why should Canfield have taken the drastic step of sabotaging their carriage? After all, what had he to fear? No one had listened to Miss Ashbourne in London. Why should he think anyone would listen to Philip, either? Or had it simply been a matter of revenge? Anger that Emily meant to marry him instead of Canfield? Or had he somehow guessed the suspicions directed at him by men like Harry? And somehow guessed that Philip was their agent. The thought made his blood run cold.

Apparently Miss Ashbourne was asking herself questions as well, for a puzzled frown creased her brow. Philip wished he could reassure her. But to speak of Canfield's reasons for what he had done, if indeed he had done anything, would mean speaking of Harry and what Harry had asked him to do. And he could not.

Softly he asked her, "Is there anywhere else we could go? Any place Canfield would not expect us to be?"

Philip waited patiently, guessing it would not be an easy question to answer. But finally she looked at him and said, a tiny frown between her eyes, "There is one place. I do not think Mr. Canfield knows of it. An abandoned cottage where we might stay."

He recoiled. "I—I meant," he stammered, "some place with people. Your reputation—and mine—would be at risk were we to go this abandoned cottage."

She shook her head impatiently. "You do not understand. There are few, hereabouts, who are not dependent upon Mr. Canfield, in one way or another. And the few who would help us, well, I will not put them at risk of his anger."

"My groom," Philip said, grasping for something with which to turn aside her plan, "we must send someone to help him with the carriage."

But she was looking past him and now nodded toward the

house with her chin. "It would appear, Mr. Langford, that someone has already come to his aid."

She was right. A man Philip recognized from the mill was pulling up in a cart with the groom by his side and the horses tied behind. As they watched, the groom jumped down, thanked the man, and untied the horses.

Philip was out of excuses. "Where is this cottage?" he asked with an air of defeat.

Miss Ashbourne gave him a speaking look and then headed off through the woods in still another direction than the one from which they came. She moved silently, no easy task when her skirts kept catching on the bushes. She solved that problem by hiking them high enough that Philip had a scandalously generous view of her ankles.

The cottage was farther away than he expected and already it was growing dark when they finally pushed open the door. It was dirty and dusty and full of cobwebs. Still, there was some wood stacked by the fireplace and the windows unbroken.

"You will be cold," he said. "I had best light a fire."

She stopped him. "I should rather be cold," she said, "than alert others nearby that we are in the cottage by the smoke from the chimney."

He nodded. She was right, of course. And had he been alone he should never have considered lighting a fire. But he found himself worrying about her and how he could protect her, whether she wished it or not.

"You will be hungry soon," he said.

"It will not be the first time," she countered. At his look of surprise she went on, "I was used to wander away from home, hiding from my governesses, and more than once found myself lost overnight. I survived then and I shall survive now. I am sorry, however, for the discomfort you must suffer, Mr. Langford."

"We shall both be sorry," he retorted grimly, "should anyone discover that we spent the night here alone."

"You forget," she said softly, with a hurt in her voice that tugged at his heart, "I have no reputation to lose, hereabouts. I was once before stranded with a man and refused to marry him. It will surprise no one when I refuse to marry you as well."

He could not bear what he saw in her eyes. Instinctively, he reached out and tilted up her chin. Gently he said, "I swear I shall not let you suffer for this."

But she pulled her head free of his touch. There was anger, now, in her eyes as she retorted, "Do give over this notion that you must forever be rescuing me! I am not a piece of porcelain to shatter at the least bit of trouble. I have never lived my life by force of gossip and I do not intend to begin now."

For all her brave words, Philip thought he could catch a glimpse of the pain behind them. He did not try again to persuade her, but merely made a private vow to do what he must to protect her.

Aloud he said carelessly, "Well, how shall we pass the time? And how soon do you think Mr. Canfield will give up searching for us?"

She hesitated, confusion evident on her face. "I do not understand why he is searching for us, in the first place. But given that he is, he won't give up until he finds us. It is not in his nature to do so," Miss Ashbourne said soberly.

That gave Philip pause, though her answer was not entirely unexpected. He paced about the room for several moments and then finally said slowly, "He will not lose interest in us unless he believes we have no interest in him. Or, rather, unless he believes I have no interest in him."

"How could you manage to make him believe that?"

Philip smiled and it was not a pleasant smile. "We cannot hope to keep our absence secret so I shall make Mr. Canfield believe that I was doing with you the very same thing that he did. I shall somehow let him know that I believed you were about to break off our betrothal and I acted to prevent you from doing so."

She colored up, but did not protest. "Yes," she said slowly, "he would believe that. And it would serve the purpose very well, I should think."

And then it seemed the most natural thing in the world to hold his arms open to her and she walked straight into them. She rested her head against the breast of his coat and said, "I promise I shall not weep but I am so very weary of this nonsense."

He hugged her tightly, knowing he ought, if he had the least sense, put her away from him. But he could not. He wanted to hold her and protect her and promise her she need never feel this way again.

And when she tilted up her head to look at him, it seemed the most natural thing in the world to bend his neck and kiss her.

It ought to have been a chaste kiss. A gentle kiss. But it became so very much more. And with a shock, Philip did put Emily away from him. He set her at arm's length and then took a step backward. And then another.

He began to pace with some agitation.

"After dark, in another hour or so, I shall take you home," he said. "And then I shall go and call upon Mr. Canfield. I shall tell him you slipped away from me and does he know where you might have gone. It will confuse him. I shall plant the notion that I meant you no good and he will believe it because it is what he would do. Then, tomorrow, we return to London before he can do any more mischief toward you."

Even as he paced, Emily came up behind him and slipped her arms around his waist. "Must we go back?" she asked.

He misunderstood. "There is no need to be afraid," he said resolutely. "He will not think to go back to your home tonight. And even if he does, you will be surrounded by loyal servants."

"I am not afraid," she answered quietly.

He turned to look at her then and was stunned by what he read in her eyes.

She ought not to be doing or saying any of this. It would put her beyond the pale should anyone ever come to know of it. But Emily could not help herself. She wanted to spend this night with Mr. Langford. With Philip. Alone. With no one to hem them about and force them to speak only conventional courtesies.

Not that there was anything conventional about either one of them. But still, she had never been alone with him long enough that they could truly speak their minds, truly share how they felt. About one another. About life. About so many things. And a night together would give them such a chance.

He was going to refuse. She could see it in his face. Nor could she blame him, for if he did stay here, with her, then he would be well and truly caught once her family knew. It was selfish to think only of how she felt and she said so aloud, then turned away.

This time it was Mr. Langford, Philip, who caught her shoulders and stopped her flight.

"I wish we could stay," he said in a voice that was husky and low. "But I will not do that to you, or to myself. One hour, and then I take you home."

One hour! So short a time. Emily wanted to waste not a moment of it. But when she risked a look at his face, she knew he would not take her in his arms again. He would not kiss her anymore, nor even touch her if he could find a way to avoid doing so.

Well, she could not blame him. Emily swallowed hard and moved away, to make matters easier for him. It was not kind to tempt them, either one.

"So," she said, with an attempt at brightness, "will you now support my cause?"

He hesitated. "I will allow that the conditions I saw were appalling. But no worse than many face on the streets of London or as chimney sweeps or such."

"Does that make it right?" she demanded hotly, forgetting, for the moment, that they were supposed to be allies.

"No, of course not. But it will not be easy to bring about change. To be sure, Lord Beaumont did seem inclined to listen. And I can think of one or two others to approach. But Emily, you must prepare yourself for the notion that change will take years, not days or weeks or months."

Emily. He called her "Emily" and seemed not to even realize he had done so. She felt a glow of warmth. Enough to let her answer equably, "I understand that change takes time. And the sooner we begin, the sooner it will happen."

He nodded, and they both fell silent. And then the rain began. Gentle, at first, then harsh clattering on the roof of the cottage. Philip stared at her in dismay.

"I cannot take you back in this!" he said.

Emily did not answer but merely wrapped her arms around herself tighter, for the temperature had begun to drop rapidly with the rain. Immediately Philip removed his jacket and put it around her shoulders.

Then he turned and began to lay a fire in the fireplace. Emily made an instinctive gesture of protest and over his shoulder he said curtly, "In this weather there will be no one to see the smoke coming from the chimney. Nor likely to come after us if they do. We do not know how long we must remain here and I will not have you take a chill."

Emily wanted to protest such high-handedness, but she could not. Already she did feel a chill and would be grateful for the warmth if they would be here for very long.

And when the blaze was burning nicely and she sat with his arms wrapped around her for added warmth, Emily admitted to herself that there were far worse ways one could spend an evening.

And when the rain kept on steadily, well past midnight,

Emily could not find it in herself to be sorry. He let her sit by his side, her head against his shoulder, and she could think of few things in the world she could want more. The cottage was dirty and cold and damp and still she fell asleep as easily as if she were in her own bed at home. Easier, for somehow, with Philip by her side, she felt utterly safe.

Chapter 21

Morning came quietly. The fire had long since burned itself out and Emily and Philip still lay together, before the now cold hearth, wrapped in every blanket they could find.

Emily woke first, as the rays of the sun peeked inside the cottage windows. It took her only a moment to realize where she was and why. Then, carefully, she disentangled herself from Mr. Langford, from Philip, and glided toward the door.

It opened silently and with one last regretful look at him, she slipped outside and headed for home. With luck, no one would ever know they had spent the night together. Philip would not need to fear any retribution from her father. Nor would he feel he needed to make amends, as she was certain he otherwise would.

Her heart was already lost to Philip. And because it was, she could not allow him to be coerced into marrying her. She had known, when he first broached the notion to her, that his heart was not engaged and it was all a ruse and she had accepted it. She could not change the rules now. Not when he would hate her if she did.

Philip woke with a groan. It seemed that every bone in his body ached and his muscles were stiff from sleeping on the floor.

The floor! What the devil was he doing on the floor? Another moment and he was awake enough to know where he was and why. And to realize that Emily was missing.

He felt a moment's alarm, afraid that Canfield had some-how managed to steal her away. Even as common sense as-serted itself and he knew that he surely would have heard such a thing, some instinct told him she was nevertheless gone. He tried to tell himself that perhaps she had just gone outside to relieve herself, but he didn't believe it.

He understood, even before he found proof, that she had gone home to protect him. To prevent him from having to marry her. And it ought to have been what he wanted. But it wasn't, Philip realized with a shock. He wanted to know that he would wake every morning with Emily at his side. He wanted to know that she would be there when he came home at night. He wanted to know that she would be there to bad-ger him during the day. He wanted, he realized, to make her his wife. To have her heart belong to him as his already did to her.

But she did not, patently could not, feel the same. Why else would she have left this morning without waking him? And left, he was certain she had.

And he was right. Emily was nowhere to be found. Philip wasted several minutes searching the area around the cot-tage. Then he noticed her shoe prints in the still muddy ground. They led straight away, as though she had not hesi-tated in where she was going. Which meant, he thought, that she had probably gone home.

He followed her trail long enough to be certain he was right. Then he veered away, assured of her safety, and headed in the direction of Canfield's property. It would be faster if he had a horse, but he could think of no way of ob-taining one that would not raise questions and suspicions. So he went on foot, recalling from the day before the way Miss Ashbourne had pointed out to him.

It took a while to get there and Philip had the lowering suspicion that his boots would have to be thrown away after

this expedition. But they got him there and although the ma-
jordomo regarded him with suspicion, he did allow Philip to
enter and agreed to ask if Mr. Canfield would see him.

Canfield, as Philip had expected, could not resist discovering why he was here. So, fifteen minutes later, Philip
found himself shown into the breakfast room and waved to
a seat and offered a plate.

"You have the look of a man who is hungry," Canfield
said affably.

"I am," Philip agreed curtly.

"You also have the look of a man who has not slept well,"
Canfield persisted.

"I didn't."

"You also—"

"I also have the look of a man who has been thwarted in
his plans!" Philip snapped as he filled his plate from the
sideboard.

That raised Canfield's eyebrows and a speculative gleam
appeared in his eyes. Still, his voice was mild as he said,
"Indeed? Care to tell me about it?"

Philip had no need to feign irritation. Or indignation. He
let both emotions fill his voice as he said, "I had it all
planned. Miss Ashbourne intended to cry off, never mind
why, and I had to prevent her." He paused and then said with
a sigh, "She made me bring her home and meant to tell her
father, here, away from all the tabbies in London. This was
my last chance to change her mind. And if my plan had
worked, she would have had to marry me. She couldn't possibly have cried off, if things had gone the way they were
supposed to go."

"But they didn't?" Canfield hazarded shrewdly.

"No, they didn't! Chit slipped the leash when I wasn't
looking," Philip grumbled. "Now she's certain to cry off and
I've nothing to show for my pains and little likelihood she'll
let herself be caught out again with me."

"None in the least, I should think," Canfield agreed.

There was silence as the two men plied their knives and forks. Then Canfield said, puzzlement evident in his voice, "I understand your ill humor. What confuses me is why you should show up at my doorstep."

Philip looked him in the eye. "Because," he said with exaggerated patience, "I am without horse and yours was the nearest doorstep."

"Ah, that explains it, then," Canfield said. "Well, I can certainly spare you one to return you to the Ashbourne household. If, that is, you think you will still be welcome there?"

It was a question. Philip pretended to consider the point. At last he sighed and let his shoulders slump as he answered, "It don't signify. I must return there in any event, as I am certain that is where my groom will have taken the horses and arranged for the carriage to be returned, once it is repaired. Besides"—he allowed himself to smile thinly— "Miss Ashbourne will not wish to advertise what occurred. I think it most unlikely that she will have told her father or aunt what transpired."

It was Canfield's turn to consider the matter. At last he nodded. "I think you may be right. No doubt she will fob them off with some other tale. Never known a girl so reluctant to be married."

He shot a keen glance at Philip then added seriously, "Whatever your reason for wishing to be leg-shackled to Miss Ashbourne, I tell you frankly that I think you are better off failing in the attempt. She will not make any man a comfortable wife. Why did you wish to marry her, anyway, Mr. Langford? And why did you have to take such measures to persuade her? I thought she liked you."

And how was he to answer that? Philip felt himself color up and decided it could only add support to his tale. If he could decide what to say, that is.

It was evident, of course, why Canfield had wanted to marry Miss Ashbourne. It would have raised his social standing, or so he thought. But Philip had no such easy answer.

He played for time. He allowed himself to seem to look wildly about the room before he settled his gaze on Canfield's face. Then he swallowed hard, straightened, and appeared to come to a decision.

"M'father wrote the most damnable will," he said at last. "A legacy to each of his sons, with none of us able to touch a penny until we marry. If we marry. And no allowance for the fact a man might have trouble finding a bride."

"You?" Canfield scoffed.

Philip shot him a sharp look. "You've not been in London much, have you?" he asked. "Or moved in certain circles. On the surface I look much the eligible bachelor. But I made a mistake. Or two. And now none of the matchmaking mamas will let their daughters near me. I thought Miss Ashbourne hadn't had a chance to learn of any of it. It seems I was mistaken. Someone opened their jawbox and told her. Just when I thought it was all set and my creditors had agreed to extend me the time I needed until after the marriage and my inheritance was mine. That's when she said she meant to break it off. She even insisted on coming back here. Well, what was I to do? This was my last chance to make her change her mind!"

The last ended on a curse and a hand thrust through Philip's dark hair. He had no need to feign the frustration he felt.

Apparently it was enough to satisfy Canfield, for he nodded. "It seems we have both been rolled up by the chit. Mind you, it would almost be worth it to see you bring her to heel. But that's not likely to happen now. Come, I'll drive you to her house."

Canfield paused, halfway out of the dining room to ask, "Why did you visit my mill with her, yesterday?"

By now Philip had himself well in hand. "Why do you think?" he demanded with a snort. "To make her believe I am in sympathy with her concerns. And because I hoped to find an excuse to delay and strand us alone somewhere."

Canfield tilted his head to one side. "So you don't care about conditions in my mills?"

"Why the devil should I?" Philip asked with a frown. "I do not expect to ever have to work in one. And even if I did, I should never be so mad as to think that anyone else would care or that I could do anything about them!"

For a moment matters hung in the balance, then Canfield nodded to himself, as though satisfied by what he read in Langford's face.

Half an hour later, Canfield set Philip down in front of the Ashbourne home. "I do hope you plan to return to London soon," the businessman said sharply.

"As quickly as I can change my clothes and my valet can pack my bags," Philip assured him. "If Miss Ashbourne will not marry me, I've no time to lose. Nor," he said grimly, "do I have a wish to be made a fool of twice."

With another curt nod, Canfield drove away and Philip slowly mounted the steps, praying that he had succeeded in allaying the man's suspicions.

Inside he found Mr. Ashbourne and Miss Ashbourne and Miss Jarrod all but shouting at one another. In spite of himself, Philip flinched.

". . . All night?" Mr. Ashbourne demanded.

"I told you, I was lost."

"Alone? Where was Mr. Langford?" Miss Jarrod asked in a quavering voice.

"The last his groom saw of the pair of you, you were supposed to be headed here," Mr. Ashbourne added sternly.

"We were lost and separated in the rain."

Miss Ashbourne appeared to have an answer for everything, but it was time to rescue her, Philip decided. He pushed open the door to the parlor and stepped inside, careful to close it behind him.

His presence immediately produced a blessed silence as

three people gaped at him. Mr. Ashbourne recovered first and advanced upon him.

"Where the devil have you been?"

Philip glanced at Miss Ashbourne who was regarding him with beseeching eyes. With a calm he did not feel, Philip said, "I spent the night in an abandoned cottage."

"Alone?" Miss Jarrod asked hopefully.

He meant to abide by Miss Ashbourne's wishes and say that he had been alone. But then Mr. Ashbourne demanded, "Why weren't you out searching for my daughter? Weren't you concerned about her welfare?"

That did it. Philip lost his temper. "I didn't have to look for you daughter, sir, because she was with me!"

That really did it. Once again three people gaped at him in stunned surprise. Then Mr. Ashbourne rounded on his daughter.

"Again?" he demanded. "What is the matter with you, that you must make a habit of such behavior? What am I to think? I begin to think you are no daughter of mine!"

But Philip could not allow Miss Ashbourne to be abused in such a way. He ignored Miss Jarrod, who kept murmuring, "Oh, dear, oh, dear."

Philip moved to stand beside Miss Ashbourne and put an arm around her waist. She tried to pull free, but he would not let her.

"I will marry your daughter, of course," he said stoutly. "You may send a notice to the papers at once. And have the banns proclaimed."

"No!"

He looked down at Miss Ashbourne. He could see the dismay, the anger, the growing horror in her eyes. Without knowing he did so, Philip smiled tenderly down at her. "We have no choice, you know. And I promise I shall do my best to make you happy as my wife."

A tear welled up in first one eye and then the other. And

began to trickle down her cheek. It tore at Philip's heart but he stood resolute.

"Surely you see this is much the best solution?" he told her, wiping away the tear with his hand.

She pulled her head back and turned her face away from him. "You do not even ask what I would wish in this!" she said in a choked voice.

"It is beyond wishes," Philip countered. "Yours or mine. But I do not think we will deal so badly with one another. We have not done so up until now."

"Up until now we have been friends, nothing more!" she countered. "Can you swear that will not change? That you will not try to rule me, once we are wed?"

Philip hesitated, taken aback. He wanted to reassure her that of course nothing would change. But he was too honest for that. With great care, he chose his words, trying to feel his way as to what he would do.

"I promise your wishes will always be paramount with me," he said.

"Not in this matter!"

He flushed. "They will always be paramount," he amended, "save when it is not in your best interests for me to agree to them."

Now her eyes were flashing with anger as she looked up at him. "And who are you to decide that?"

"I will be your husband," he said stiffly. "It will be my duty to make such decisions. For the both of us."

Now she did succeed in completely breaking free of him. Emily backed away, her fists clenched at her sides. Her voice was wild as she flung her words at him.

"Now do you wonder that I never wish to marry? It is because of just such arrogance as yours! You say you will consider my wishes, but only when they do not run counter to yours. No, I tell you! I will not marry you. I will not marry anyone. Let me be a spinster, like Aunt Agatha. I shall be far happier than as a slave to some man's mind!"

Philip went white. His own fists clenched at his side, though he was not conscious of it. He had no answers for her, for her words were so outside of what he knew to be right and proper and sensible.

Nor could her father do more than remonstrate by saying her name over and over again. "Now, Emily! Emily!"

It was left to Miss Jarrod to answer her. The older woman, who had, at one point retreated to the farthest corner of the room, now came toward her niece. Her own voice was hot with anger as she spoke.

"So you wish to follow in my footsteps, do you, Emily? Well, consider them well, for you would have even fewer advantages than I do! You would be always dependent upon the charity of your male relatives, of whom there are very few. Always at their beck and call when you are allowed to stay in their homes. Never having all of the necessities of life, and surely no luxuries."

She paused and drew a deep breath before she went on, "Even I, who was left a competence by my father, was not allowed to set up household on my own. Consider, Emily! Do you truly mean that you would rather be whispered about and laughed at than be the wife of a man who would treat you with kindness and consideration? You will not even try to see if there is a way to reach a contract, of sorts, between you? You will not even try to see if he might be amenable to change or to listening to what you wish to say?"

Now it was Emily's turn to go very pale. She flinched at each question flung at her. And when Miss Jarrod was done, she took a step toward the older woman and held out her hand.

"I never knew you were so unhappy," she said.

Miss Jarrod shrugged irritably. "And I was to tell you? And have you worry over something that was neither your fault nor in your power to correct? I think not!"

"Listen to her!" Mr. Ashbourne said hastily. "Agatha makes a great deal of sense, Emily."

With a sense of desperation, Philip said in a voice that was not altogether steady, "Perhaps you could let me talk with Miss Ashbourne alone? I know it is not entirely conventional but—"

He got no further before Mr. Ashbourne snapped, "Why not? You have already done something far more improper than that! And if you can talk some sense into my obstinate daughter, you will have my eternal gratitude, Mr. Langford. As well as her hand in marriage."

And then, without another word, Mr. Ashbourne stalked from the room followed by Miss Jarrod, who walked away with a back held ramrod straight and a pinched look on her face.

When they were alone, Philip regarded Emily for a long moment without speaking. Finally he asked, his voice humble, "Would it truly be so terrible to find yourself leg-shackled to me?"

She would not meet his eyes but traced, instead, the pattern on the back of the chair behind which she had taken refuge. And for a long moment she did not answer. He began to think she never would.

But then, abruptly, she looked up and met his eyes with a steady gaze of her own. And then she said those damnable words, "I don't know."

Chapter 22

It was most unfair of him to ask her such a question, Emily thought. Particularly when she wanted so desperately to agree. The thought of waking every morning to find him beside her, to going to sleep every night in the same bed, to be with him during the day, to lie in his arms, to be held and kissed, was so appealing, that Emily could not imagine anything she could possibly want more.

But marriage? Place herself forever in his hands? She could not bear the thought! What if he changed? Or she did so? He was asking only out of duty, not because he cared for her as she cared for him. And that made what he asked impossible.

If Philip loved her, then love might temper his tendency to autocracy. But he did not, and so he would have no reason not to bend her to his will just as he wished. Already he had tried to do so more than once. No, it was a future that Emily could not, would not accept.

So when she answered, it was in a clear, steady voice as she said, "I don't know."

"Emily!"

His voice was shaken, distinctly shaken. Perhaps that was a good sign? Still, Emily made herself continue in the same cool voice as before.

"Why? Why do you wish to marry me? You need have told my father nothing."

For the second time that morning, Philip tried to find an

acceptable answer to that question. Only this time he wasn't seeking a lie Canfield would believe, but the truth in his heart, a truth that he hoped would be acceptable to Emily. One she would not instantly reject. And that was far more difficult.

"I love you."

She gave a most unladylike snort of disbelief. "Easy to say," she told him. "But most difficult for me to believe. Why? How could you possibly love me?"

He met her eyes squarely, even as he took her hands in his. He gazed down at her, oblivious to the tenderness in his eyes as he said honestly, "I don't know why. Or how. You are difficult and unconventional and will no doubt land me in the briars any number of times. And if I had the least sense I would run the other way as fast as I could."

She stared up at him, her own gaze unwavering and he took heart as he went on, "I don't know why I love you, Emily. I only know that when I look at you I want nothing more than to take you in my arms. I want to hold you, protect you, and be forever your friend. I want you to laugh with me and fight with me and I want to spend the rest of my mornings seeing you across the breakfast table."

Then, because he could think of nothing else to do, Philip let go of her hands and opened his arms wide. She hesitated only a moment then, miraculously, she walked straight into them and put her own arms around him. Even as he hugged her tight against his breast, she clung to him fiercely.

She turned her face up to his and when he bent to kiss her she made not the slightest protest. Finally, when he somehow found the strength to let her go, he took a step back and held out his hand to her.

"Will you marry me?" he asked in a voice that was not nearly as steady as he would have wished.

She swallowed hard, then slowly reached out her hand to take his. "Yes," she said.

For a long moment they clung to each other. Then, with a

ragged laugh, Philip said, "I suppose we had better tell your father."

She nodded, not trusting herself to speak. But there was no need, for apparently her father and aunt had been listening at the door.

"Ah, well, well, so that's all settled, nice and tight," Ashbourne said, beaming as he came into the room, rubbing his hands together.

Even Miss Jarrod was smiling, albeit a trifle tremulously. "Do you mean to be married soon?" she asked. "Or do you mean to return to London to finish ordering your trousseau?"

Emily was about to refute the notion, when she realized Aunt Agatha was blushing! Abruptly she changed her mind and said innocently, "Well, if Mr. Langford does not mind waiting, a short while, before we are married, I should like to purchase a few new things in London."

"Whatever you wish," he said promptly.

Emily's father would have objected, but apparently decided he had best not risk making matters worse. "Well, so long as Mr. Langford is in London with you, I suppose it will do no harm," he reluctantly agreed.

"I shall be by her side, every possible moment!" Philip promised recklessly.

"Of course, I will need you to accompany me, as well, Aunt Agatha," Emily said innocently.

Miss Jarrod blushed even more and did not try to hide her happiness at the thought. "I shall go upstairs and give orders for our things to be packed at once," she said.

"Here, now, that's for Mr. Langford to say, when you will leave," Ashbourne protested.

Philip wanted to tell them that the sooner the better, so far as he was concerned. But he couldn't. There was still work to be done. The workers had said the uniforms would be ready by tonight and that in a day or two would be sent on their way. He had to take action tonight. But he could not say so to Emily or her father or her aunt.

As Philip hesitated, trying to decide what to say, Ashbourne forestalled him. He cleared his throat and looked sharply at Philip. "You'll leave tomorrow morning, at the earliest," he said sternly. "For this afternoon, you and I have marriage settlements to discuss."

Philip bowed, entirely undaunted. He even managed to smile reassuringly at Miss Jarrod and wink at Emily. Then he followed Mr. Ashbourne to the study.

That left Emily and Miss Jarrod alone.

"And just why are you so eager, Aunt Agatha, to return to London?" Emily asked.

Miss Jarrod looked everywhere but at her niece. "I, that is to say, well, oh, the devil with it! I wish to see Sir Thomas Levenger again. I think it quite possible he may come up to scratch, if I do!"

Emily blinked in surprise at her aunt. It was not simply the woman's use of cant, though that was extraordinary in itself, but also that her aunt was quite serious about the matter and willing to say so aloud.

Miss Jarrod held herself stiffly, as though expecting laughter or teasing or some expression of exasperation. Instead, Emily threw her arms around her aunt and kissed her cheek.

"I hope he may do so!" she exclaimed. "And if he does, I hope you will accept him and that the two of you will be very happy together."

Emily felt Aunt Agatha tremble and she stepped back. There was a tear or two glistening on her cheek. Miss Jarrod hastily swiped it away.

"Thank you, dearest Emily," she said in a voice that quavered with emotion. "And I wish you every happiness with Mr. Langford. I do think he is a good man and will make you happy, if it is within his power to do so."

Again Emily felt a sense of unease. But there was no use

repining over the matter. If her marriage was not what she wished, why then she would simply have to make it what she wished. And if Mr. Langford thought he could prevent her, he would soon discover he was mistaken.

With that thought, Emily felt much better and she and her aunt finished making their preparations for the morrow's journey.

In the other room, Philip regarded Mr. Ashbourne steadily. "I will not be bled," he said. "My inheritance is sufficient to support a wife and I have every intention of making her a generous settlement. But it will be placed in her hands."

"But are you certain you do not at least wish to invest in my stables?" Ashbourne persisted. "I will have only the finest breeding stock. It will be a capital success. All I need are the funds to begin."

"Funds that will not be coming from my pocket," Philip retorted grimly. At the sight of Ashbourne's crestfallen face, however, he sighed and said, "Perhaps I know of someone who would be willing to invest in your scheme. It goes against the grain for me to recommend it, but I will speak to him when I return to London."

Ashbourne was dismayingly grateful. He grabbed Philip's hand with both of his and pumped it up and down.

"Thank you! Thank you! Neither you nor this other person will regret it! I shall go make a go of things, I shall!"

Philip took leave to doubt it, but he did not say so aloud. He did not ask why, if Ashbourne could make a success of such a thing, he had not done so before his funds ran out. The man was, after all, his bride-to-be's father.

But it was as though Ashbourne anticipated him, or even read his mind. He let go of Philip's hand, poured them both a drink, and said, handing him a glass, "I would have done this on my own, you know, if my father had not left the estate so encumbered. Gambling debts. Had to sell off the best of my horses the moment I learned the extent of the damage. It's taken me twenty years to clear the worst of those debts. But somehow there's never been enough to become so beforehand that I could set up the stables as I wished."

"Why not mortgage the land?" Philip asked with a frown.

"Because we don't own it," Ashbourne retorted bluntly. "Emily don't know it, but I had to sell it, early on. No other way to keep us out of debtor's prison. But the new owner agreed to let me live here for the rest of my life. For a reasonable rent, of course. But he's kept the arrangement secret, and for that I am grateful."

"Why would he do that?" Philip asked.

Ashbourne shrugged. "Thought I'd pop off early, no doubt, given how heavily I was drinking back then. And later on, he began to drop hints about how, when Emily was of age, perhaps he could marry her. Keep everything in the family, so to speak."

"Canfield!"

Ashbourne nodded. "Never thought Emily would take so against him as she did. Never thought he'd go to such lengths to force her hand."

"What will happen now?"

Ashbourne stared into his glass for a very long moment. Then he raised bleak eyes to Philip. "Don't know," he said. "I've the contract that says I've the right to stay here until I die, but I don't know whether he'll try to drive me out or not. I may hope not, for it would look very bad, hereabouts, if he were to succeed. Canfield's greatest ambition is to be accepted as one of us, as a gentleman. And gentlemen do not do such things to one another."

Philip hesitated, then, against his will he said, "If you are thrown off your land, sir, you may come to Emily and me and we shall make certain you always have a home."

"Dashed if you aren't a good fellow!" Ashbourne exclaimed. "Like you better than Canfield, I do. Like you much better. Even if you won't invest in my stables."

*   *   *

Canfield heard the news by evening. He was both puzzled and angry, wondering how Langford had managed to pull off the trick. He also wished Langford joy of his new bride-to-be. She was a hoyden and a termagant and altogether unlike any lady he had ever known. Let Langford deal with her fits and starts and tempers. He was well rid of the impetuous creature!

The thought, however, which cheered Canfield the most, was that Miss Ashbourne would no doubt soon discover her bridegroom was not quite what he seemed either. If any man could handle the girl, he suspected it was the barrister. And she would so dislike being handled! That thought improved Canfield's mood so greatly that he was able to smile and tuck into his evening meal with a fine appetite.

Mind, he would still need to look about him for a bride, and perhaps even go farther afield than this county. But all in all, that might not be entirely a bad thing. Perhaps he should go to London for a Season. There must be some, among the men he dealt with discreetly, who would help him gain the entrèe to some of the homes of the gentry.

Deep in thought with his new plans, Canfield wasted no further time or energy on the question of Miss Ashbourne or Mr. Langford. He had other fish to fry.

The new uniforms were finished and some set aside to be sent on to France in the morning. With luck no one would notice the diversion of one special lot. Or if they did, they would not speak of it to anyone who mattered. No one ever had before, why should they now?

Chapter 23

Philip thought he was going to be able to sneak out of the house alone and unseen. He ought to have known better. Emily slipped up behind him as he was saddling a horse to take him to the mill.

He whirled at the sound and found himself face-to-face with a very determined-looking young woman. She was wearing a riding habit and clearly prepared to accompany him.

"Go back in the house," he said.

She shook her head. "Whatever you mean to do at the mill, you will manage better if you have my help."

"How did—"

Emily regarded him wryly. "For all your efforts to keep me uninformed, you must have guessed that my friends at the mill would tell me you were coming back there tonight. Why?"

Philip silently and rather bitterly reflected on the changing mores that allowed a young lady to so bluntly quiz her fiancé. And to ignore his wishes.

He tried charm. He tried bluster. In the end he was forced to tell her at least a little of what Harry had told him about Canfield and the uniforms.

"So you mean to find out if he is shipping them to the French?" Emily asked slowly.

"I mean to do more than that," Philip countered. "With the help of your friends, I've thought of a way to mark the uniforms that are to be sent on to French. If we can be sure those are the ones. That way, every man wearing such a uniform can be easily checked to see if he is a spy or not."

She smiled. "Then I had best come with you. There will be a great deal to do and very little time to do it in. You will need my help persuading them. Come, my mare is already saddled."

And if Philip had been confounded before, he was even more so to discover that Emily had been able to manage such a task without his hearing a thing. It was very fortunate, he thought, helping her into her saddle, that it was Harry and not he who engaged in cloak-and-dagger stuff on a regular basis.

They tied up their horses some distance from the mill and went the rest of the way on foot. As promised, several workers were waiting to open the doors to them. There was no doubt they were pleased to see that Emily was with Philip.

He raised his eyebrows in surprise. "Canfield doesn't keep his mill locked?"

One of the workers grinned. " 'E thinks 'e does but keys can be copied, they can."

"And locks picked," another chimed in.

Philip looked around but they were already inside the building and the door closed behind them.

"No light shows from outside," one of the men said, guessing his concern. "Now, what does a fancy toff likes you wants wif us?"

So Philip explained. About the uniforms. And what he wanted. They knew. The workers knew which uniforms had been set aside to be sent out special. And when it was likely to happen. Within minutes they were at work, carefully stitching on the inside in a place that would be unnoticeable to the wearer.

Emily and Philip kept guard. They also talked with the workers so that by the time the job was done, Philip had an even better sense of why Emily was so upset by conditions in the mill and his mind was planning whom he would approach when they returned to London.

Finally the uniforms were all marked and the workers slipped, one by one, out of the mill. Philip and Emily were among the last to leave. They made it to their horses unseen and he helped her up. Then, as quietly as they could, they set off down the road toward her home.

They didn't speak at first, both too tired and, now that the job was done, a sense of constraint between them. But Emily finally broke the silence.

"Will it work, do you think?"

"I must hope so, for my brother and all the men who are fighting with him," Philip said soberly.

"What about Canfield? Will nothing happen to him?"

Philip thought about not telling her, but in the end he feared she would just follow him again if he did not. "After I have seen you home, I mean to go back and watch the mill. Someone thought it possible Canfield is having the uniforms fetched in the morning. Early. I mean to be there to see it. I shan't stop them, but I shall follow as far as I can and then return to report back to my brother."

To his relief, she didn't argue. Instead she said thoughtfully, "We shall not be able to leave in the morning for London. I shall have to fob off Papa and Aunt Agatha with some excuse. Perhaps I shall have a headache."

In spite of himself, Philip grinned. "You are the most complete hand!" he said. "And I've no doubt that after we are married you shall lead me just as merry a dance as you've led your father and your aunt all these years."

Completely unabashed, she grinned back at him and said, mischief in her voice, "I mean to try!" Then, more soberly she added hesitantly, "Do you mind? Having to marry me? You made such a pretty speech, this morning, about loving me, but did you really mean it?"

Instantly Philip reached out to grab the reins of her horse and pull it up short next to his own. In a voice that even to his own ears sounded fierce, he said, "Never think that I had to marry you! I wish to marry you. I love you. I meant what I said. I know you do not feel the same, yet, but I shall try to make you happy. No, it is you who I fear is being forced into things."

Was it shyness he saw in her eyes? Some other emotion? Tears? And then her hand was over his, pressing tightly, as tightly as her voice was pitched as she said, "I do want to marry you, Philip. I love you. Indeed I think I have loved you since the first day you took me home."

Were it not for the urgency of his mission, Philip would never have been able to find the strength to let go of her reins. "We'd best get you safely home now," he said, "and safe. But be assured, we shall continue this again at another, better time."

She let go his hand and they were once more riding down the road. Philip let her go the last stretch alone, watching from the road until he saw her turn into the stable yard and slide down from her horse. Then he turned and rode back toward the mill.

The weight in his pockets reminded Philip of the things he carried on Sir Thomas Levenger's advice. False papers. False maps. And a pistol. Philip cursed the weight of all three in his pockets.

He could still hear Sir Thomas's voice telling him, "You don't know what you shall find. Canfield may be passing on more than uniforms. Maps or battle plans. Carry false ones to place in their stead. And remember that he may be on his guard and you will find the need to defend yourself. Carry a pistol, m'boy!"

Never mind that Philip hated pistols. Never mind that he could not recall when last he had fired one. Yes, yes, that was one more charge of ungentlemanly conduct to be held against him by George, but he hated the blasted things and he could feel this one slapping against his thigh, in the pocket of his coat, as he rode.

Well, if it went off by accident, it would be Sir Thomas's fault. And he would curse him not only now, as he rode, but to his face as well. Still, Sir Thomas had been right just often enough, in the strangest of circumstances, for Philip to be unwilling to ignore his advice.

Philip only hoped it would prove wise tonight.

Canfield took the papers out of their temporary hiding place, wrapped them carefully in sharkskin, and then finally rolled them tight within one of the uniforms. He paused as he thought he heard a sound, but it did not come again and he decided he had been mistaken. It was beginning to get foggy outside and that always distorted sounds. Or perhaps it was a rat. There were certainly enough of them running around this place at night.

He had more important matters to worry about. The men would be here soon. Everything had to be ready. They did not like to be kept waiting and Canfield was not about to cross men who looked as these did. He never saw the shadow that followed him as he took the bundled uniforms outside. Or moved closer when a group of very unsavory-looking men appeared.

Canfield and the men moved a short distance away, to discuss payment and a few other matters. None of them noticed the shadow stealing up to the uniforms or the exchange that took place. Or saw it slip away again before the men moved to collect the bundle of uniforms and place it at the bottom of their farmer's cart.

Canfield did think he overheard the sound of an extra set of horse's hooves following the wagon carrying the uniforms and the men who meant to deliver them. But he shrugged it off as a trick of the fog that had descended such a short time before. Besides, the sound was moving away. If there was a problem, let the men in the wagon deal with it. He had no doubt they could do so. In any event, it was cold and late and he wanted to return home to his nice, warm bed.

*   *   *

It was later, many hours later before a very weary Philip could rest. He rode into the yard of the inn, where he knew Harry was staying, awaiting word from him, as exhausted as the horse he sat on. And he slid from the horse's back as eager for food as the loyal creature who had carried him so many miles in the night.

Inside, the innkeeper, already rising for the day's work, readily agreed to provide him with a private parlor but looked much taken aback when asked to wake a guest at this ungodly hour. But there was no need. A soft step on the stairs and Philip turned to see his brother Harry coming down in his stocking feet, boots in hand.

They clasped hands in silence then followed the innkeeper to the promised private parlor. Harry ordered a hearty breakfast for both of them and silenced the innkeeper's protest at the earliness of the hour by tossing him a gold coin.

"You look much in need of something to restore you," Harry said when the man was gone.

"I've ridden far tonight," Philip agreed grimly. "I'm sorry, Harry, but I lost the men before they reached the coast. Lost them in a little village called Halingdale. I'd forgotten it was market day and by the time we reached there, probably around four o'clock in the morning, the blasted place was already full of wagons coming to market. I got cut off and by the time I managed to make my way to the center of town, the men and the cart had disappeared. I asked after them and tried to look about but it was useless, I'm sorry."

Harry nodded. "Clever of them. But in any event, at least we know for certain now that he is sending uniforms to the French."

"Uniforms and something else," Philip added.

From his pocket, Philip pulled the papers he had abstracted and replaced with the false set he and Sir Thomas had concocted between them. He gave these papers to Harry, who whistled softly.

"You'd best tell me the whole story," Harry said.

Philip did so, leaving nothing out, including Levenger's advice and the news of his own betrothal. Harry's eyes lit up at the description of how the uniforms had been marked— cunningly so that no one was likely to notice, but easy enough to spot if warned.

By the time his recital was done, interrupted only when the food was brought in, Harry's eyes were dancing and he was grinning with unmistakable approval.

"Excellent, Philip! I could not have done better myself. Are you certain you would not wish for a post with the military? We could use a man with talent such as yours."

Philip smiled at his brother sardonically. "I thank you, no. Tonight's excitement was more than enough for me. I am quite content with my law books and cases in court."

Harry shrugged. "A pity."

For several moments they ate in companionable silence. Then Harry said, "Tell me about this Miss Ashbourne. I have heard James's opinion and George's and even Athenia's. But from what you have told me tonight, she sounds a remarkably resourceful woman and one I should like. Tell me more about her."

With a wry smile, Philip did so. And by the time he was done, Harry was grinning. "She sounds just the wife for you, Philip, whatever George may say. I look forward to meeting her. But now I must be on my way back to London."

Both men rose to their feet. "What will you do?" Harry asked. "Sleep? Return to London with me? I must get these papers to the ministry without delay."

Philip shook his head. "I must return to Miss Ashbourne's home and hope that she has somehow managed to conceal my absence. That or account for it in some plausible way. We were to start for London this morning but that, patently, is impossible now. I must hope, presuming her father does not withdraw his consent to our marriage, that we will start for London tomorrow. Will you still be there when I get back?"

Harry nodded slowly. "Yes, and your public pronouncement of your betrothal will be my signal to wash my hands of you and return to fighting in Spain. It will answer very well, I think."

"I am so glad that my betrothal suits your plans," Philip replied with heavy irony.

Harry only laughed. "I hope she will lead you a merry dance, brother. From everything you have said, it seems inevitable that she will do so and it will do you good."

Philip hesitated then asked, "You do not mind that I have broken our pact? You and James and I, never to marry?"

Harry merely made a rude sound in reply.

Another brief silence then Philip said, "What will happen to Canfield?"

"Nothing. At least not for some time. Probably six months at the very least. By then the French will have begun to realize that the uniforms are a liability, not an asset. And that the papers they received were false. If they do not do something about Canfield, then the ministry will. Why?"

Philip hesitated. Then, slowly he said, "I think that I may find myself buying a mill. In about six months or so."

Harry gave a shout of laughter. "That will please George, it will! Miss Ashbourne's influence, I presume?"

"Go to the devil!" was Philip's sour reply.

Harry laughed again. He did, however, have one last piece of advice and he spoke it soberly. "I should avoid Canfield, if I were you," he said. "You would appear to have successfully fooled him as to your purpose. But you do not wish him to connect you to what has happened, should he discover that something has gone wrong."

"Believe me, I mean to stay as far away from Canfield as possible," Philip replied in the same serious tone. "Although I should think his mind would be on his grievance with me in the matter of Miss Ashbourne, no more than you do I wish to see him warned as to what we have done. And I fear I should find it hard to pretend to knowing nothing after what I saw and did tonight."

"Good."

Harry nodded curtly. It was time for the two men to go their separate ways. They exchanged a few more words, then Harry tucked the papers into his own pocket and headed for his room to pack. Though in truth he had, as always, traveled very lightly.

Philip went out to the stables and called for his horse. He was sorry to have to push the creature any farther, but there was no help for it. This was Ashbourne's horse and while his own absence could perhaps be explained away, the disappearance of a horse, to be replaced with another, would not be so easily done.

So Philip rode, hoping that Emily had been as clever with her tongue on his behalf as she so often was on her own.

When he finally rode into the Ashbourne stable yard, he found Emily's father cursing out the stable hands for letting him take a horse and be gone all night.

"There you are! Out drinking and sowing the last of your wild oats, I've no doubt!" Ashbourne exclaimed.

Philip managed to stagger a bit and speak in a voice that seemed a trifle unsteady. "About to be married. Can't do so afterwards."

Ashbourne snorted. "Of course you can! Just need to be discreet. Well, well, no harm done, I suppose, so long as my Emily doesn't catch sight of you like this. Come, I'll show you the back way into the house. We'll nip up the servant's stairs and I'll have your man sent up to you. Sleep for a few hours and you'll be right as a trivet and none the wiser. But tomorrow you leave for London. I'll not take the chance of my Emily changing her mind yet again. The sooner I see the pair of you buckled together, the better I shall feel."

Meekly, Philip allowed himself to be led inside.

Chapter 24

It was late by the time Philip has seen Miss Jarrod and Emily settled back into their hired house in London.

Philip's first task the next morning, however, was to call upon Sir Thomas and thank him for his assistance. He was welcomed warmly. And then they got down to business.

"Right, was I?" Sir Thomas asked.

Philip nodded. "About Canfield passing on battle plans with the uniforms, yes. Here, by the by, are the maps we did."

He started to hand them back to Sir Thomas, who held up a hand to forestall him. "Keep them. You may need them at some point in the future if my reading of Harry's character is correct. And I suspect it is."

He paused then looked at Philip and said shrewdly, "Well, have you decided? Are you going to marry Miss Ashbourne, after all?"

"Yes."

"No need to color up, m'boy, I think it's an excellent notion."

Philip leaned forward, a smile on his own face that Sir Thomas Levenger profoundly distrusted. He was quite right to do so.

"You approve of matrimony, then, do you, sir?"

The older barrister nodded warily, not willing to commit himself with actual words.

It was, nevertheless, enough for Philip. His voice was

soft, but with an edge that betrayed his springing of the trap. "If you approve, sir, then why don't you get married yourself?" he said.

For once Sir Thomas found himself without words to reply. He gaped at Philip. He started to stammer. He started to cough. Finally he glared and said, "You are an impertinent puppy, Philip!"

The younger man leaned back in his chair and smiled at Sir Thomas, not in the least abashed. "Am I? But if the institution of marriage is such a worthy one, why do you avoid it, sir? Particularly when there is a lady who would be very happy to become your wife."

For a moment, Philip thought his mentor was going to have a fit of apoplexy, so dark did his complexion become.

"You do not know what you are talking about!" Sir Thomas thundered.

Philip merely smiled. "No? Perhaps not, but I'll wager Miss Jarrod does."

Sir Thomas began to fiddle with some papers on his desk. He avoided Philip's eyes. "Miss Jarrod has been kind enough to dance with me, I'll grant you that, but it is a far cry from considering someone an eligible dance partner to being willing to consider marrying that person."

"Not so far for her," Philip answered softly. "She speaks of you with great affection and I know that she has told Miss Ashbourne that were you to offer for her, she would not refuse."

Sir Thomas's head snapped up and his eyes met Philip's sternly. "If this is some sort of jest—"

"It is not, sir, I assure you."

Something that Philip could only believe was hope seemed to fill Sir Thomas's face. Still the older man stammered and blustered a bit, but in the end he merely said quietly, "I suppose Miss Jarrod and Miss Ashbourne are on the Ashbourne estate?"

"No, sir, they came back to London with me."

"Where are they staying?" Sir Thomas asked diffidently.

"The same place as before. It seems Miss Ashbourne hired the house for the entire season."

Philip gave him their direction, just in case he did not already have it. Then, without haste, he rose to his feet and said, "I know you will excuse me, sir. I know you must have things to do this morning and so do I."

"Yes, yes," Sir Thomas said, somewhat absently.

Philip left his mentor's office feeling very satisfied with his morning's efforts.

A short time later he was meeting with his man of business. "Yes, a mill," he said gently but firmly. "It is not yet for sale but I have reason to believe it will be. At that time I wish you to purchase it."

"And, er, when do you believe it might become available for purchase?" the harassed fellow asked.

"Perhaps in five to seven months," Philip replied.

The man made an attempt to bring Philip to his senses. "You have, sir, a reasonable competence, but I am not at all certain it will extend to purchasing a mill!" he said severely.

"I have reason to believe this one will come very cheap."

The man pressed his thumb and forefinger against the bridge of his nose. "And if it does not?"

Philip shrugged. "I am certain I can find others who will back me in this."

The man spread his hands. "But why?" he asked, almost pleading.

Philip smiled to himself. "It's to be a belated wedding present to my wife," he replied.

The man gaped at Philip. "A wedding present?" he echoed, his voice squeaking in disbelief.

Philip's smile broadened. "Yes, a wedding present. I am certain I can leave the details to you. Simply inform me when the matter is done."

"Yes, sir. I most certainly shall," the man of business said, speaking in precisely the sort of tone one might use to humor a madman, which his expression left no doubt he thought Philip was.

Undaunted, Philip rose to his feet and went on to his next rendezvous. He found his brother James still in bed and insisted that his valet rouse him.

By the time James came into the breakfast room, belting a robe angrily about his waist, Philip was tucking into a generous portion of ham with which the valet had kindly provided him.

"What the devil is the meaning of calling at this ungodly hour?" James demanded.

Philip looked at him and gestured toward a chair. "There is no need to shout. Have some ham, it will improve your temper greatly."

"I don't want to improve my temper," James grumbled, but he sat nevertheless and allowed himself to be given some of the ham.

After Philip was certain his brother had calmed a bit, he said lightly, "I came for two reasons. One was to tell you that the news of my betrothal to Miss Ashbourne should be in the papers tomorrow."

"Good. I like the girl. Sensible creature, unlike most of them," James said, mildly enough.

Thus encouraged, Philip went on, "And the second reason is that I have a request for you. I should like you to design safer equipment for a mill I expect to be buying within the year."

James looked up, understandably more surprised by this than by the other bit of information. Still, he merely lifted his eyebrows and said, "Intend to set up George's back, do you?"

Philip shrugged. "It cannot be helped. But I do not mean for him, or anyone else, to know, if possible."

James nodded. Philip waited and when his brother did not speak, he began to drum his fingers on the tabletop. When even that did not provoke a response he finally said with pardonable exasperation, "Well? Do you mean to help me or not? I should have thought you would enjoy the challenge of designing such machinery."

James ate, without any apparent hurry, the piece of ham on his fork then said, "Already am." At Philip's look of surprise, James added, "Your Miss Ashbourne asked me, the night of Lady Jersey's ball. Happy to oblige."

"But how did she know that you do such things? No never mind," Philip said, holding up a hand. "I suppose she ferreted it out of you." He started to chuckle and then it turned into a full-fledged laugh. James joined him, the corners of his eyes crinkling in amusement.

"You are the most complete hand!" Philip exclaimed, getting to his feet. "I ought to have known that Miss Ashbourne would already have managed to corrupt you. Very well, I shan't press you for details. Time enough for that when and if I do possess the mill. For now I shall leave you to your breakfast. I have a great deal to do this morning."

James merely smiled and watched his brother leave.

That only left George to inform. And Harry since he was not, officially at any rate, supposed to know what had passed during Philip's visit to the country. And, per his instructions from Harry, Philip sought out his brothers at White's.

George seemed please to see him. Harry hung back, watching, prepared for the fireworks he knew were about to explode.

"There you are, Philip! Back from the country already? Good, good. Knew you'd see reason," George said heartily.

Philip clapped his older brother on the shoulder. "Oh, I'm back. And I thought it best to tell you myself, before the news hits the papers tomorrow. Miss Ashbourne and I are to be married. You may wish us happy!"

George looked as near to apoplexy as Sir Thomas had done some time earlier. "But—that is to say—Athenia assured me . . ."

Now Harry patted his oldest brother on the shoulder.

"The words you are looking for are congratulations and I wish you happy," Philip prompted.

Lord Darton glared at his brother. "Well, of course I do," he said. "It is just that I do not agree with you on how it might be achieved!" He paused and changed his tone. "Surely you see this is impossible?" he pleaded.

"No, George, I do not," Philip said stiffly. "Harry, you agree with me, don't you? Tell George that the match is unexceptionable."

There was a twinkle in Harry's eyes, but he had a role to play. This was, after all, the reason he was supposed to be in London—to try and prevent just such a mèsalliance. So now he avoided Philip's eyes. He looked down. He looked at the tar wall. He looked at his impeccably groomed fingernails.

Finally, with an exaggerated sigh, Harry said, "Oh, the devil with it! It is your life, Philip, and I must suppose you know what you are doing. I wish you congratulations and hope that you shall be very happy." He leaned closer to Darton and said, "Think, George! The matter is clearly settled. If you wish to have any prayer of avoiding scandal, you had best try to put a good face on the matter."

Darton grumbled, but even he could see the sense of that. Finally he clapped Philip on the shoulder and said roughly, "Well, I don't say that I like it but you are old enough to know your own mind. I do hope you shall be happy with the girl, I just don't depend upon it."

"That is quite enough for me," Philip retorted with a wry smile "I should not expect more from you." He turned to Harry and asked, "How soon do you return to duty?"

Harry glanced at Darton and there was a wry smile on his face as well as he replied, "I suppose, under the circumstances, there is nothing to keep me here any longer. I shall probably leave London in the morning."

A look passed between the two brothers and then Philip took his own leave knowing that behind him White's would be abuzz with word of their encounter.

Then, finally, he headed for his office. There was a great deal of work to catch up on.

It was hours later before he was free to call upon Miss Ashbourne. The first words she said when Whiten showed him into the drawing room were, "Aunt Agatha and Sir Thomas are getting married!"

Philip looked over at the older couple, who were blushing. Murmuring suitable words of surprise and approval, Philip greeted both of them.

"I shall wish you happy, sir. And Miss Jarrod, I can only hope that Sir Thomas realizes how fortunate he is."

Sir Thomas growled but there was no doubt he was also pleased. "I do, you infernal puppy!" he said. "Now go out to the garden with Miss Ashbourne and plan your own wedding! Your future household. How many children you wish to have. Anything, so long as you leave Agatha and me alone."

Philip grinned. "An excellent notion!" he replied, smiling warmly at Emily.

He offered her his arm and she took it, blushing sweetly. And they went, as Sir Thomas had directed, out to the back garden to plan the rest of their lives.

Epilogue

Philip stared at Emily warily over the breakfast table. She had that glint in her eyes that warned him she was planning something she knew he wouldn't like.

He was right.

"Philip, my friend Lady Cathcart says that she is going to take a tour of Bedlam today. You don't mind if I go along, do you?"

Philip closed his eyes for a long moment, then opened them again. He fixed his gaze firmly on her face. "Bedlam? What are you planning to do? Loose the residents? Attack the guards? Lecture the director? Tell me the worst, Emily. What are you planning now?"

She had a look of injured innocence that fooled neither one of them. "I just thought," she said, tracing a design with her fingertip on the tablecloth, "that I might gather some information."

"Information?" Philip raised an eyebrow and his voice was skeptical as he said, "To what purpose, my love?"

Now she grinned at him. "Well, I did think an article or two in the paper might stir things up a bit. Provide a call for change. Particularly if people know that at times even ladies have been placed there."

Philip sighed. "The conditions at Bedlam are no secret. Not when anyone can tour the place and laugh at the residents anytime they wish," he pointed out.

"Yes, but by the time I am done, they shan't laugh," she

said seriously. "I shall waken their sympathies. And their indignation. And if it isn't real, well, they shall be afraid to admit to it by the time I am done."

His lips twitched with amusement. Philip had no doubt she could do it. Her articles, published anonymously, were the talk of London. Everyone wondered who the fiery young man was who was writing them. Only Emily, Philip, and her editor knew the truth and Philip devoutly hoped it would stay that way!

"I suppose," he said with an exaggerated sigh, "that this means you will soon be asking me to take on the case of one of these unfortunate creatures, imprisoned there?"

Her eyes lit up. "I hadn't thought that far ahead, but of course! It would answer perfectly."

Philip groaned and wondered silently why he had been fool enough to give her notions. "Oh, no," he said. "They are already calling me the reckless barrister!"

Emily read his expression perfectly. She came around the table and hugged him. "You are merely a good man who cannot bear to see injustice done, any more than I can."

"Don't think to come over me so easily as that," he growled.

She kissed his neck, right below his ear. "I don't," she whispered. "But it is very hard to pretend to be heartless when I know you purchased Canfield's mill and gave it to the workers to run."

"It was an excellent investment," he countered.

"And was it an investment when you paid half the salary of the servants you hired for Aunt Agatha and me when I first met you?" she asked, kissing his neck below the other ear.

"You weren't supposed to know about that!"

"But I do."

"You will be the ruin of us both, one of these days," Philip warned.

Then, with another groan, he turned and pulled her onto

his lap. "I won't have you forever turning my life upside down!" he said, frowning as severely as he could.

Emily wound her arms around his neck and said, "I know."

And then, before he could say anything more, she kissed him. Not a chaste salute, but a kiss of depth and passion that made them both forget everything else and Philip found himself thinking that having such a wife—one with passion in her heart—was not, perhaps, such a terrible thing after all.

And if, because of her, he was known as the reckless barrister, well, perhaps that was not such a terrible thing after all, either. Somewhere, he thought, his father was probably smiling.

Author's Note

Look for James's story next, *The Wily Wastrel*. Appearances are deceiving as this apparently frippery fellow tries to hide his natural genius for invention from his disapproving older brother, Lord Darton. He has no interest in the silly young ladies who are forever being paraded before him as possible wives. But what happens when he meets a young lady with a mind as fine as his own?

I love to hear from readers. Please contact me via email at april.Kihlstrom@sff.net.

Or write to me at:

Box 240
532 Old Marlton Pike
Marlton, NJ 08053

Please enclose a stamped, self-addressed envelope for a newsletter and reply.